"Don't analyze every word I say

Mollie didn't mean to be snappish, but having Flynn constantly around was making her tense. "Look, I'm sorry. If it means we'll find the manuscript, I'm willing to be an amoeba under your microscope."

Flynn's gaze roamed over her body. "You're much too shapely to qualify as a one-celled organism."

"Not to mention I'm much too tall."

"I like tall women. They generally have great legs."

"You're a leg man, huh?" Mollie teased.

Flynn smiled wickedly. "Don't get me started. I'm trying my best to keep my analysis confined to your words and not your body."

"Good," she said quickly. "Because my body is definitely not part of our arrangement. Trust me—I don't have a treasure map tattooed on my—"

"Don't even say it." Flynn gave an exaggerated moan and pulled her into his arms. "Don't even say it...."

Cassie Miles 's quiet hometown of Denver, Colorado, was recently invaded by the rich and famous of Hollywood. The sequel to a popular action-adventure movie was being shot there, and the entire town showed up for extra work—and the chance to be a star. But Cassie was too busy writing about the rich and famous to join the fun. Cassie's sixth Temptation is about the children of famous people and how the fame—or notoriety—of their parents affects their lives. Cassie explores this powerful theme in a fast-paced love story that combines glamour, intrigue, suspense . . . and passion.

Books by Cassie Miles

HARLEQUIN TEMPTATION
104–IT'S ONLY NATURAL
170–SEEMS LIKE OLD TIMES
235–MONKEY BUSINESS

HARLEQUIN INTRIGUE
122–HIDE AND SEEK

Don't miss any of our special offers. Write to us at the following address for information on our newest releases.

Harlequin Reader Service
901 Fuhrmann Blvd., P.O. Box 1397, Buffalo, NY 14240
Canadian address: P.O. Box 603,
Fort Erie, Ont. L2A 5X3

Under Lock and Key

CASSIE MILES

Harlequin Books

TORONTO • NEW YORK • LONDON
AMSTERDAM • PARIS • SYDNEY • HAMBURG
STOCKHOLM • ATHENS • TOKYO • MILAN

Published July 1990

ISBN 0-373-25405-9

1

"WOODROW LOCKE, the great American poet and writer, was larger than life and twice as mean."

Eighty-seven-year-old John Marscel hunched over the podium like a praying mantis and glared at the black-tie crowd assembled in the Chicago Hyatt Regency banquet room. "Woody was a brawler who could outfight, outdrink and outwrite anybody. Though he's been dead these past thirteen years, his talent has endured. Ladies and gentlemen, Woodrow Locke is a legend."

Mollie Locke clenched her fists beneath the linen cloth covering the head table. Being the only child of someone famous was difficult enough; being the daughter of a legend was nearly impossible.

Why would John Marscel, her godfather, say such a thing? He'd always been opposed to the glamorization of the arts. Mollie leaned toward Claudine Marscel, who was seated at her left, and whispered, "What is your husband plotting?"

"A surprise," Claudine murmured.

"Swell." Mollie hated surprises.

"You must learn to relax," said Claudine in her melodic Parisian accent. "This tension is not good. You are only twenty-nine years old."

There were days when Mollie wished she could relax and be like Claudine, who was still elegant and utterly feminine in her late sixties. But this was not one of those days. At this banquet, Mollie knew she must keep her guard up.

"You need a man," Claudine deduced.

"I'd prefer a tranquilizer."

Mollie inclined her head to create the impression that she was paying attention to Marscel's speech. A surprise? Oh, great! Her thick brown hair grazed her bare shoulders. She'd chosen a strapless gown for this occasion—fire-engine red as a warning: Keep away from me! No trespassing!

Unfortunately, her warning hadn't worked too well. Throughout dinner, a parade of scholars had approached her and inquired if her presence meant that she was finally willing to grant interviews about her father. It did not. Mollie refused to discuss her life with her father. Not now. Not ever. Not until the moon turned mauve and the Chicago Cubs won the World Series.

"As executor of the Locke estate," Marscel continued, "I'm here to accept the Tilton Literary Award on Woody's behalf."

He held up a slim volume. "This recently published book—*Gateway*—is a collection of love poems written by Woody to his third wife, Ramona. These were letters. Not meant for publication. Not his best work. So, why honor him for *Gateway*? Is it because you eminent scholars have no taste? Or perhaps your award is an apology for an era when the anemic academic community disdained a man who acted like a real man."

He flung the words like a challenging gauntlet. But no one picked it up. There were no dissenting murmurs or clatterings of silverware to insult the ferocious old man.

Mollie's stomach wrenched. She knew the silence would infuriate Marscel. He hated being indulged. More than once, he'd gruffly stated that respect was for funerals.

"By God, I miss you, Woody." Marscel bent his tall frame and picked up his wineglass to sip the blood-red Bordeaux. Then he gestured to the vacant chair at Mollie's right. "I had intended to introduce you to Dr. Flynn Carlson."

"I'm here!" came a shout from the rear of the banquet hall.

A tall, blond man strode between the tables, and Mollie watched him curiously. Throughout the banquet, Claudine had spoken of little else but Flynn, which she pronounced "Fleen." Fleen was *très* amusing, *très* intelligent, *très* handsome.

As Mollie peered through the semidarkened room, she decided that Claudine's eyesight must be fading. *Très* handsome? He was tall, moved athletically and had a swarthy macho tan, but his features weren't classic. His eyebrows were too thick. His nose was crooked. He was rugged, maybe. But not an Adonis.

"I'll introduce him on the run," Marscel said. "Dr. Flynn Carlson teaches English at Bowdoin College. He's the author of three novels of suspense and has just begun research on a biography of Woodrow Locke."

A biographer? Mollie shuddered and looked away. She was bored to death with being courted for information about her father, the legend.

Claudine nudged her arm. "Do you like Flynn?"

"He's not my type."

Flynn approached the head table. He hadn't planned to be late, but he wasn't disappointed to have missed a dull awards dinner. He'd come only because Marscel insisted and because he wanted to meet Mollie Locke.

He took the empty chair on Mollie's right, nodded to Claudine, then focused on Mollie. Her head was turned away from him, politely listening to Marscel. Flynn studied the pattern of freckles on her shoulder and the flicker of light through her hair. Though he'd seen her in photographs, those had been pictures of a little girl. And Mollie was very much a woman. He leaned forward for a better view. The delicate spray of freckles directed his gaze down her throat to the swell of her breasts. A fresh clean scent as pure as sunlight in the morning emanated from her hair.

When he touched her arm, she recoiled, then swiveled around to glare. Incredible eyes, he thought. "You're Mollie Locke."

"Yes." Quickly she added, "And you're a writer. I should warn you that I never discuss my father."

"When he wrote about you, he called you 'Green Eyes.' Now, I understand why."

Her jaw tightened. Her amazing eyes narrowed. With a regal turn of her head, she deliberately looked away from him.

At the podium, Marscel announced, "I have a surprise, ladies and gentlemen. As executor of Locke's estate, I have decided that Flynn will write the first officially authorized biography of Woodrow Locke."

A civilized grumbling from the audience greeted this announcement, and Mollie saw Marscel's satisfied smirk. She'd been right to dread this surprise. Marscel was trying to stir up controversy by appointing a man with less than sterling credentials to this coveted position.

"It's going to take the finesse of a lion tamer for Flynn to handle Woody's ex-wives." Marscel nodded toward

Mollie, "Not to mention this little green-eyed tiger—Woody's daughter."

Mollie blinked the aforementioned eyes. Little? Mollie was almost five feet ten inches tall. Definitely not little.

"Let's take this opportunity," Marscel said, "for these two young people to formally meet. Flynn and Mollie, come up here and shake hands."

When Marscel stepped back from the podium, Mollie tried to demur. Why should she stand up? She wasn't a literary great. Not a legend. Yet she couldn't tactfully refuse when Flynn pulled her chair and directed her toward the microphone.

Every eye in the room was on her. Mollie could feel their cold intellectual scrutiny. And she had the nightmare sensation that she'd forgotten her clothes and stood naked for all to see. The direct appraisal in Flynn's eyes raised goose bumps along her bare arms and reinforced her vulnerability. Even in her two-inch-high heels, she had to look up to confront him.

When he took her hand in both of his, the touch banished her chill, replacing her nervousness with the heat of anger. He seemed to be teasing her. Then he winked. The man really was insufferable, talking about her eyes and winking as if she were some bimbo who was waiting to tumble into his arms.

"I look forward to interviewing you for the biography," he said.

"Do you? Well, Dr. Carlson, you'll be looking for a long time and a long distance. You might need a telescope to see that far into the future."

"No farther than Venus. Can we meet tomorrow?"

"I'll see you on a space shuttle first."

"That could be arranged. Tomorrow? At NASA?"

Their exchange had been picked up by the microphone, and the crowd responded with laughter. Flynn didn't miss a beat. He raised their joined hands high in a victory salute.

Mollie didn't bother to be subtle when she ripped away from him, pivoted and returned to her seat. What an ego! His arrogance was unbelievable.

"A handsome couple," said Marscel as he returned to the microphone. His chuckle became a cough, and Mollie saw his fingers tremble slightly as he again reached for his wine.

Immediate concern for her godfather overcame her anger. Marscel was too excited, flushed. Should she stop him from speaking? Insist that he sit down?

This was her fault. She should have blocked the publication of *Gateway*. During the past few months, the strain on Marscel had been tremendous. Renewed interest in her father had sparked requests from the most exalted literary critics to the sleaziest of tabloids—each one grasping for a piece of Locke's epic story. And John Marscel was the executor of her father's estate, the keeper of the flame.

Marscel pulled himself upright. "Ladies and gentlemen, I'm wondering how you'll take this next bit of news."

He paused dramatically. Was he all right? Must be, Mollie thought. He was well enough to pick a fight, to tease the crowd.

Marscel announced, "I have decided, after careful consideration, to open Woodrow Locke's private papers exclusively to Dr. Flynn Carlson."

A collective gasp burst from the gathered scholars and patrons of literature. Locke's private papers! In his position as executor of Locke's estate, Marscel had consistently refused to allow Locke's correspondence, journals and notes to be studied. The only exceptions were personal letters that had been saved, like Ramona's love letters, which she compiled as *Gateway*.

The focus on Flynn intensified to such a laser-edged glare that Mollie almost pitied him. Long ago she'd learned that academics were not above infighting. The possibility of a literary discovery caused the intellectuals to swarm from their ivory towers like a flock of vampire bats. For years they had been sucking at her with their questions: What games did you play with your father? Did you know about his infidelity to your mother? Did he teach you to swim? To hunt?

Now Flynn Carlson would be their target. He probably deserved it. After all, he was no better than the others—just another Ph.D. writer trying to make his reputation from the legend of Woodrow Locke.

"I haven't gone senile," Marscel said into the microphone. "I know that Flynn's doctorate is not from a prestigious college. His publications have been in popular fiction, not academic journals. But he has other qualifications. He's a mountain climber. He built his own sailing craft. Off the coast of Florida, I saw him ride bareback on a dolphin. Though Flynn never met Woodrow Locke, I know he'd have Woody's approval. Still, I suppose you're wondering, 'how dare Dr. Carlson presume to take on this task?'"

Flynn dared. He expected protests from his colleagues, especially since he did not plan to paint a scholarly biographical portrait. Flynn wanted to portray Woodrow Locke, the man. Not the legend.

Initially he hadn't sought to be Locke's biographer. All he'd wanted was to satisfy a curious itch. The paradox was that Locke had been an obsessive writer who was capable of turning out a finished manuscript in less than six months. Yet he'd published only seven novels and ten slim volumes of poetry during his thirty-year career. Had there been other books? Flynn wanted to know what secrets were hidden among Locke's private papers.

Over a year ago, he'd met with Marscel and Claudine and had fought to see the private papers. Of course, Marscel refused as he always had done. But Flynn was persistent.

Then, surprisingly, a genuine bond developed between Marscel and himself. They went sailing together, fishing together and spent several long nights arguing. During one of those nights, Marscel made his decision—he wanted the true story about Woodrow Locke, and he decided that Flynn was the man to tell it.

"That's settled," Marscel said, leaning against the podium. "Now I'm going to tell you a story about Woody. You've probably all heard this before, but I'm an old man and I guess that gives me the right to bore the pants off you."

Marscel launched into a famous anecdote about the time Locke was elk hunting and got lost in the high Colorado Rockies. When he returned, after five days of exhaustion and exposure, Locke didn't ask for food but for paper. He immediately sat down and wrote five perfect poems.

Midway through Marscel's story, Claudine reached across Mollie to touch Flynn's arm. She whispered, "I worry for Marscel. He is too excited."

Flynn could see she was right. Marscel was supporting his weight on the podium. Obviously he was overwrought. But Flynn also recognized the stubborn pride of this old lion. Marscel wouldn't give up the podium until he was good and ready. "It's his story, Claudine."

"But he is killing himself. Can you not see?"

"Woody was a man's man," Marscel concluded. "And the best damn fisherman I've ever known. There was the time when . . ."

The high scarlet in Marscel's cheeks faded to a pallor that emphasized the dark hollows beneath his eyes. The old man's gaze was wistful, as if peering down a dark tunnel of memories toward that bright moment when he would be reunited with his old friends.

"Stop him, Flynn," Claudine pleaded.

Flynn left his seat and went to the podium. "Thank you," he said, slapping his hands together to start the applause.

Marscel growled. "I'm not done."

The staid academic crowd finally reacted. They had been goaded enough for one evening. A husky professor who was also seated at the head table stepped forward. "Sit down, Flynn."

"Nice to hear from you," Marscel said. "Flynn, this is Dr. Edleman. He wrote a book that was formerly considered the definitive Locke biography."

Flynn extended his hand, and Edleman ignored it.

"Who do you think you are?" Edleman snapped. "You don't deserve to look at those papers."

"That's right," came a shrill from the floor.

Mollie glanced down from the head table in horror. A renowned poetess charged at the head table in a flurry of paisley silk. "Flynn is a cheap suspense writer," she shouted. "I should be the one who sees Locke's private writing. Only someone like me could understand his tortured genius."

"You? Don't make me laugh." A tuxedoed man with a British accent stormed to his feet. "You couldn't understand the first stanza of a nursery rhyme."

Claudine went to the microphone. She took her husband's arm. "Please, Marscel. You must not be so excited."

"I'm fine."

He was beaming, and Mollie could see that these outbursts suited Marscel. It wasn't respect that he demanded. It had never been respect. She knew what the old gentleman sought—the thrill of a fight. A damn good fight. She stepped up beside him. "All right, Marscel. That's enough. You've had your fun."

"A fitting tribute." He chuckled. "Your daddy would have loved it."

He was probably right.

"Ladies and gentlemen," Marscel boomed into the microphone. "Do you think I'm being unreasonable?"

"Yes," came a chorus.

"Should I donate Locke's papers to a library?"

There were "yes" and "no" answers. Not a consensus.

"I suppose you think that the private correspondence should be open to everyone. But that's not how it's going to be. I won't have anyone painting Woody Locke as a sainted genius. Or as a tragic sinner."

Heated protests rumbled through the ballroom, drowning out Marscel's final triumphant statement. "It is with great pleasure that I, as executor of the Locke estate, accept the Tilton award for *Gateway*, a posthumous collection of Woodrow Locke's previously unpublished poetry. I thank you."

He hoisted a glass of wine. "Here's to you, Woody." Marscel drank and hurled his empty wineglass against the wall behind the head table. It shattered.

Before the shards of crystal had stilled, Edleman reached past Flynn to grab Marscel's arm. "You can't do this to me."

"Back off," Flynn warned.

The burly professor pivoted and confronted Flynn. Though the two men were the same height, Edleman outweighed Flynn by a good fifty pounds. "You go to hell, Flynn."

Edleman lashed out. His fist nearly connected with Flynn's jaw, but instinct caused Flynn to duck. When Edleman swung again, Flynn caught his hand in midair, then released his grasp, allowing Edleman's forward momentum to drive him away from the podium.

Edleman staggered, got his bearings and bellowed, "You're mine, Flynn. Get over here."

Flynn peeled off his tuxedo jacket and tossed it onto a vacant chair. To Mollie, he explained, "It's rented. I don't want to wreck it."

Around Mollie was a clamor of voices. Everything was horrifyingly out of control. She needed to stop this noise, this rampant confusion. But how? Behind her, at the podium, the president of the Tilton Literary Society pleaded with the dignified crowd to behave properly.

Mollie caught Flynn's arm. "I'll give you an interview. If you don't fight, I promise that I'll give you an interview."

"You will?" His blue eyes sparked into hers.

"Yes." She heard the crowd beginning to settle. "Yes, if you come right now and sit down."

Edleman yelled, "Don't hide behind Mollie. Come on, Flynn. Woodrow Locke never in his life walked away from a fight."

"He's right," Flynn said sadly.

"But you're not my father."

"Come on, pal," Edleman challenged. "You've got to prove to me that you deserve to see those papers."

"He's not going to stop," Flynn said. "I'm sorry, Mollie. I have to do this. But I'll be quick."

He squared off with Edleman. Flynn threw the first punch, a hard blow to the belly that doubled Edleman into a knot.

With that blow, Mollie felt the air whoosh from her own lungs. Damn Flynn Carlson. She hated him and all the macho myths he stood for. "A brawler," she remembered Marscel saying of her father. "He could outfight, outdrink and outwrite . . ."

A scream pierced the hubbub.

Mollie whirled and saw Claudine on her knees beside her husband. Marscel had collapsed.

"Help him," Claudine sobbed.

Mollie rushed over. This was her fault. She should have known. A banquet honoring her father couldn't have turned out any other way. She shouldn't have allowed Marscel to speak. She had been blind to the warning signs.

Flynn was beside Claudine. He neatly removed Marscel's necktie, unfastened his starched collar and prepared him for CPR.

Weakly Marscel pushed at Flynn's hands. "Let me be. I want to go. It's time, my turn."

"No!" Mollie fell to the floor beside him. "You're going to be fine. Don't leave us."

He sighed. "You're a grown woman, Mollie. Stop blubbering."

"Yes, sir." Mollie fought back her tears.

Marscel looked up at Flynn. "A good fight, wasn't it?"

"If I'd known what you were planning, I'd never have . . ." He stopped himself, gazed into the old man's pain-filled eyes and sighed. "It was a damn good fight, Marscel."

"Edleman?" Marscel queried.

"Sore," Flynn replied.

Marscel's grin was weak but contented. His breathing seemed to steady as he looked up at Mollie. "I was right about Flynn," he said. "And about you, too."

"Of course." She didn't have the vaguest idea what he was talking about, but Mollie reassured him. "Don't talk now. You need to save your strength so you'll be all right."

"Yes. I'll stick around for a while longer." His voice trailed off, "Don't want to miss the next good fight."

2

MOLLIE LEANED BACK in the swivel chair behind her desk. Slowly and clearly she spoke into the telephone receiver. "I am not fighting. I'm simply stating the facts."

"Fine. When can we meet? I'm in Chicago."

Mollie stared up at the acoustic-tile ceiling in her office at Onadime Office Supply. Couldn't Flynn Carlson get it through his thick skull? "We will not meet. I have done all the interviews I intend to do. Ever."

"Those weren't exactly in-depth, Mollie. Anybody would learn as much by reading Edleman's biography."

"Please don't call me again."

She slammed down the receiver. It had been two months since the banquet when Marscel had collapsed from exhaustion and a minor heart attack. Two grueling months. And Mollie—trying to protect Claudine and to obtain a small measure of privacy for Marscel—had unwillingly stepped into the limelight. After she'd stated a few facts and closed with "no comment" a million times, the demands of reporters and scholars had finally subsided to a whisper. Except for Flynn.

He had grown louder and more persistent. And now he was here in Chicago? Flynn was the last man on earth she ever wanted to see. The official biographer of Woodrow Locke. The person who was guaranteed to rake up questions she didn't want to face.

Shuffling a stack of invoices into her "out" tray, she reviewed her neatly typed itinerary. Next week she'd be on the road, making sales calls in southern Illinois and introducing a junior rep to several of her long-term accounts. Though she would communicate with her office, it would be easy to evade Flynn. Why did he keep calling anyway?

"The Marscels," she muttered in answer to her own question. Claudine and her cantankerous husband kept shoving Flynn in Mollie's direction. Their matchmaking was about as subtle as a neon sign. Claudine had practically painted a big red *A* for *Available* on Mollie's chest.

And why was Claudine so convinced that Mollie needed a man? Never had Mollie been the sort of woman who yearned for a male shoulder to lean upon. She was employed full-time, had an excellent credit rating, a company car and a mortgage on a Tudor-style town house in the west Chicago suburbs. She did charity work with neglected children. People depended upon her. Mollie was so brilliant at taking care of herself that she could easily juggle the problems of several other people.

Leaning forward, she picked up her phone and buzzed the receptionist. "Gretchen? That was Dr. Carlson on the phone. Again."

"Was it? Oh, Mollie, I'm really sorry."

Mollie detected a false note in Gretchen's apology. It was probably safe to assume that Flynn had somehow charmed the sweet but ditzy receptionist into disregarding Mollie's instruction about holding his telephone calls.

"If he calls again," Mollie warned, "do not under any circumstance put him through."

"But what should I tell him?"

"Tell him I do not wish to speak to him. Really, Gretchen, that should be obvious."

"Okay. Whatever you say."

She sounded hurt, but for once Mollie didn't care. Though she and Gretchen were the only women in the nine-person executive sales department, there were limits to sisterly camaraderie.

"By the way, Mollie. You have a meeting in five minutes. Conference Room B."

"I know that."

Mollie disconnected the intercom. A meeting? She grabbed her calendar. The page for today was completely blank. She hadn't made note of any meeting.

Dammit, she was losing it. She'd always been super-responsible on the job, never misplaced her receipts, had an exemplary closing ratio with her accounts and hadn't taken a vacation in three years. Yet suddenly she couldn't even remember a lousy meeting.

Damn. She grasped a crystal paperweight and drew back her arm to throw. In her mind's eye, she saw the paperweight hit the smooth beige drywall with a satisfying thud. With trembling fingers, she set the crystal sphere down on her desk and sank back in her swivel chair, staring blankly, shivering. What was wrong with her?

During the past two months, she'd been hounded by a steady stream of pests seeking the definitive story on Woodrow Locke. There were reporters lurking behind every potted palm tree. Photographers with telephoto lenses. She'd even received a proposal of matrimony from one desperate scholar who wanted the rights to her memoirs. Damn *Gateway*. And damn Ramona for publishing her father's letters.

But that was mostly over now. Why hadn't her tension passed? If anything, Mollie felt worse, incapable of handling everyday details. Her temper had been on a hair trigger. She'd cursed people who didn't use their turn signals in traffic. She'd snarled at a grocery store clerk who shortchanged her by four cents, and yesterday she'd nearly wept at the dry cleaner when she picked up the red dress she'd worn to the banquet.

Mollie had always prided herself on being calm, cool and collected. Now—much too often—she was sobbing, shrieking and shattered. What was happening to her? She hadn't fallen apart on either occasion when her parents died.

Offering a shrug for the absurdity of life, Mollie decided that she must be losing her mind. Her father, after all, had not been a paragon of sanity. Must be that genetics had finally caught up with her. Like father, like daughter? No way.

She hefted the paperweight. Her father would have thrown it. He would have laughed when it smashed through the wall. But she had been able to maintain control. Mollie shook her head and grinned. She wouldn't have been able to throw it properly, anyway. As her father always said, she pitched like a girl.

Slipping her white linen suit coat over her navy blouse, she took a stack of manila folders from her desk. Though she had no idea who she was meeting or what it was about, she could fake it. With purposeful strides, she passed Gretchen's desk.

"Good luck, Mollie," the receptionist called out.

Luck had nothing to do with it. Hard work and control were the keys to a happy, productive life.

She whisked into Conference Room B. The room appeared to be empty. Though she could see only the high back of the chair, she knew someone was sitting at the end of the long conference table. But who? Who was she supposed to be meeting? She set down her files with a thud. "I'm here," she said brightly.

The high-backed chair swiveled around. "Hello, Mollie."

Her mouth dropped open when she beheld Flynn Carlson. He flipped open a briefcase on the table, took out a sheet of paper and came toward her. Instinctively she took a step backward. "What are you doing here?"

"I stopped by yesterday. You were out, so I wrote a note of this meeting on Gretchen's calendar."

"Gretchen," Mollie muttered. She would kill Gretchen. Right after she murdered Flynn.

"Don't blame the receptionist," he said. "She was away from the desk when I did it."

"But I talked to you on the phone only a few minutes ago. How did you get here so fast?"

"Let's call it a technological marvel." He smiled then admitted, "I called from the lobby downstairs."

Before she could raise any further objection, he handed the paper to her. "Read this."

"I will not." She set the note on the table and slid it back toward him.

"Come on, Mollie. Don't be rude."

"After all your uninvited phone calls? How dare you talk to me about courtesy."

"I know your schedule is free right now. Take a minute and read this note. If you're still not interested in listening to me, I'll be delighted to bow out of your life."

Flynn's blue eyes held hers. Playing hide-and-seek with Mollie Locke wasn't his idea of a good time. Though she was beautiful, he suspected that she was a spoiled brat— one of those attractive ladies who delight in leading men around by the nose and who always manage to get what they want.

He slid the note back toward her. "I found the original among your father's private papers."

In spite of herself, Mollie was intrigued. "The documents that Marscel kept sealed for the past thirteen years?"

He nodded. "Marscel and I have been going through them. There are reams. When your father wasn't writing poetry or novels, he must have been jotting notes or firing off letters. But, of course, you know that."

Mollie picked up the letter and read the sprawling handwriting. It was to Marscel about ski conditions in Colorado during January of 1968. Mollie was seven years old at the time.

The last paragraph read:

"Well, old friend, I've finished it. Turned out to be longer than expected. 346 pages of my finest work. This one is for my darling Mollie, my green-eyed girl. Someday, when she dares to follow the charted rhythm of her heart, she will find this—my treasure."

Mollie looked up. "His treasure?"

"A manuscript. There are subsequent references to 'his treasure' and a story for Mollie. And several bits of further documentation that lead me to believe this 'treasure' was never published."

Flynn watched her for a betraying signal, an indication that she knew about this lost work of Woodrow Locke.

"Don't stare," she said. "It's impolite."

"You look a great deal like your father."

"No, I don't. My eyes are wider apart and my chin isn't square. I'm nothing like him."

He threw up his hands to ward off her hostility. "Whatever you say. Just tell me about this note. Did your father ever tell you about a book he'd written especially for you?"

"No comment."

"I'm not trying to trick you into an interview. The possibility indicated by this note is far more exciting. Think about it. There could be a missing manuscript— a completed novel—from Woodrow Locke."

"You don't need to make it sound so terribly important."

"It is important."

"No, Flynn. A cure for cancer is important. Fighting against famine is important. Preserving the environment is important. Another novel from Woodrow Locke is merely. . . interesting."

She stalked out of the conference room. By the time she reached Gretchen's desk, Mollie had built up a fuming head of steam. While the receptionist juggled three phone lines, Mollie stood waiting—grinding her rear molars and waiting. A quick death was too good for Gretchen. Mollie intended to kill her slowly.

"Mollie," Gretchen bubbled, "this call's from New York. It's Claudine Marscel."

"Oh, swell." That was all she needed—friendly advice from Claudine. She exhaled loudly. "I'll take it in my office."

Whirling around, she saw Flynn. Before she could tell him to get out of her life, he said, "Don't worry. I'll be waiting right here."

In the privacy of her office, she clutched the telephone receiver like a lethal weapon. "What is it, Claudine?"

"Mollie, you sound upset. Did Flynn locate you?"

"Yes, he did."

"But then, you must be so very pleased," Claudine said. "To think of it, Mollie. Your papa wrote this book especially for you. It is marvelous."

"I'm glad you think so."

Yet, as Mollie listened to the story of how Marscel and Flynn had located the letter and had compiled other corroborating information, she was happy to hear the enthusiasm in Claudine's voice. Marscel's collapse and subsequent recovery had been hard on her, and it was a relief to hear her godmother chattering away in a bright mixture of French and English.

"... and, *certainement*, you and Flynn will find this treasure, this masterpiece."

"Excuse me, Claudine? What are you talking about?"

"The search, of course." She gave an earthy laugh. "This Flynn, he is a handsome treasure-hunter, *n'est-ce pas?* I think, maybe, you will like him very much."

Mollie shuddered. Going anywhere with Flynn was not a wise idea. Joining him on a treasure hunt for a manuscript that might not even exist sounded like borderline insanity. Why not save time and call the men with the straitjackets right now? "I have a question. Why hasn't Marscel mentioned this missing masterpiece to me before?"

"Ask him yourself."

Mollie groaned as she heard the telephone being passed from bubbly Claudine to her acerbic husband. Double trouble.

"Mollie," came the gruff, commanding voice of John Marscel. "You go with Flynn and help him."

"How are you feeling?"

"Bored. The damn doctor says I have to stay in Manhattan. No travel. Or else I'd come with you and Flynn."

"Flynn and I are not going anywhere."

"Sure you are. It's high time you found this missing manuscript. It's my guess that Woody hid it. You know how he got suspicious of people in his later years."

"The word is paranoid," Mollie said.

"It's my guess that he wrote this book only for you and didn't care if it got into print. He wanted you to have it when you were old enough to understand."

Though she readily accepted the idea that her father—during a full-blown attack of paranoia—had stashed a manuscript somewhere, Mollie had a hard time believing that it had anything to do with her. "If this thing exists, why haven't you looked for it before now?"

"I have. Don't you remember that trip we took to the Florida Keys?"

"Yes, I do." About a year after her father's death, she had gone with Marscel to her father's hacienda. They made a thorough, step-by-step search. But Mollie dismissed it as an attorney's fussiness about paperwork. "You never mentioned a missing manuscript."

"Of course not. You were only sixteen, Mollie. I was afraid you might tell someone else about it. Can you imagine the furor that would have caused among our effete intellectual pals? Hell, they would have ransacked the damn house."

This was beginning to make sense. Except for one thing. If she hadn't been able to discover a hiding place before, how could she find it now? "Is this manuscript in Florida?"

"Who knows. I'm guessing he left some kind of clue with you—that business about following the charted rhythms of your heart."

"But I don't remember any kind of clue."

"You need to remember." His voice was serious. "I'm speaking as your godfather now. You need to make peace with your past. It's eating away at you."

Mollie recalled her tension over the past few months, her sudden attacks of weeping or shouting. More than likely, her anxiety had something to do with her father. But why exhume the past? She'd done very well for herself by ignoring it, and she did not want to sift through the bloody remains. Better to keep it hidden. If she could.

Marscel continued, "You've never been keen on talking about your father. Never answered my correspondence about your estate. You've never drawn a penny from the trust fund."

"I don't need it." She brushed away Marscel's accusations. Her father's estate was the single inefficient area of her life. Whenever she received a document, she filed it, unopened. "Why now, Marscel? Why should I search now?"

"Because of Flynn," he said. "With your memories and Flynn's determination, I'd give good odds on your chances of finding the manuscript."

Flynn. With a jolt, Mollie recalled the man who was at this very moment hovering outside her office door, luring Gretchen down the primrose path toward inefficiency.

"Give him a chance," Marscel said. "You'll like him."

Impossible. He was everything she disdained: an adventurer, a professor and a writer. Flynn caused shudders of horror to creep up and down her spine. "Sorry, Marscel. I have to refuse."

"Reconsider, Mollie. This is important to me."

His voice held a pleading note, and she was shocked to hear it. She'd known Marscel since her birth, and he'd never asked her for anything. This manuscript must be deeply significant for him. "Why is this manuscript so important?"

"I hated *Gateway*," he said. "And I hate the idea that it was the last of Woody's books to be published. He deserves to be remembered for something better than a bunch of half-finished love letters to Ramona. If you won't do this for your father or for yourself, Mollie, do it for me."

"I'll think about it. But I won't promise anything." Except, of course, that she'd feel guilty for the rest of her life if she didn't at least try to find this manuscript. "Say *au revoir* to Claudine for me."

She hung up the telephone and quickly formulated a plan: confront Flynn directly and honestly. Insist that she needed time to consider. Tell him she would contact him later. She grabbed her purse and sailed through the door.

When she neared the reception area and saw Flynn perched on the edge of Gretchen's desk, grinning and flirting, Mollie's decisiveness faltered. He winked at Gretchen, and she didn't hesitate to bat her eyelashes in return. *Winking*, Mollie thought. He'd winked at her during the Tilton award banquet, and she'd given him a cold shoulder in return. These simple male-female games baffled her.

Flynn's blue-eyed gaze caught hers, and she announced her plan. "Marscel informs me that you intend to search for this alleged missing manuscript and you want me to help."

"Correct."

"I will give careful consideration to your proposal, Flynn, and I'll contact you later with my decision." She turned to Gretchen. "I'm going to lunch."

Flynn rose to his full height. It was frustrating that he could tower over her. "May I join you?"

"Suit yourself."

When Mollie marched away from him, she forced herself not to look back. There was no reason for him to join her. She hadn't given him a shred of encouragement. No kind words. No fluttering eyelids. Not even a wink. By now he must have deduced that they were not simpatico, and that was fine with her. If he backed off, she wouldn't have to bother with this treasure hunt.

Boarding the elevator, she turned and saw Flynn standing beside her. Perhaps she should have been annoyed, but her lips twitched in a perversely happy smile.

"How's Claudine?" he asked.

"*Fantastique.*"

The elevator descended. "Listen, Mollie, even if you don't care about the literary value of this manuscript, it could be worth millions. Look at the success of *Gateway*, and that was nothing but a bunch of average poems."

"I don't need the money," she said. They exited into the lobby. "Besides, the royalties on my father's books are an attorney's nightmare—what with his ex-wives and the 'friends' he left things to."

"This would be all yours. There were papers, in your father's handwriting, indicating that his novel, entitled *The Key*, is yours. One hundred percent. Marscel has already taken care of the legalities."

"*The Key*," she murmured. Something clicked in her mind, a distant memory. *Locke's key.*

"Do you remember the title?" Flynn asked.

"Not really."

Flynn and Mollie stepped into the dense humidity of a Chicago summer. It was lunchtime, and the sidewalks were jammed with pedestrians. Nobody dawdled in the city, and the skyscraper canyons reverberated with thousands of voices and footfalls.

Mollie had always thought that the streets of Chicago were a wonderful place to be alone. The anonymity provided a rare moment of solitude. Today, however, she wasn't by herself, and there was something oddly comforting about the presence of the tall man who strolled beside her.

"In some of his notes," Flynn said, "your father indicated that you might have some idea of where to find his treasure."

"He also said, during the last years of his life, that he'd discovered Bluebeard's hoard. He hid out in a mountain cabin for two months in the mid-seventies because he thought Hitler was after him. He claimed to have wrestled an alligator."

"Can you remember a special place?" Flynn persisted.

"No."

"Possibly you accidentally stored the manuscript with some of his other mementos."

"I don't keep souvenirs from my father." She'd never had much use for his old fishing hats or stuffed animal heads or empty gin bottles. "I'm not sentimental. Anything he gave me went to the estate, and I'm sure Marscel would have noticed a manuscript."

They headed east, past State Street. Near Lake Michigan, the sky widened above them in a hot white haze. Though there weren't enough clouds to rain, it wasn't clear enough to see the sun. Mollie walked quickly. A drop of sweat trickled down her collarbone and between her breasts. "May I remind you, Flynn, that I have not agreed to participate in your search."

"Consider this." They stood on a corner, waiting for the green light. "Back at your office, you mentioned some causes you thought were important. A Locke manuscript would make a ton of money. Think of all the whales you could save."

"No comment."

But he was right. A missing manuscript from her father was a guarantee of big bucks. Though her personal finances were comfortable, she could imagine the stunning impact of a giant donation to Outreach for Kids, the child welfare organization where she donated a good portion of her time.

Outside the Art Institute, the crowds thinned, and Mollie detoured from the stream of pedestrians. She strolled halfway up the stairs and paused beside a stone lion who snarled from his sun-sparkled pedestal. "You know that Marscel and I searched the hacienda in the Keys and found nothing, don't you?"

Flynn nodded. "He told me."

"Why would this attempt be any different?"

"Two reasons. One, since Marscel never mentioned the manuscript, you never knew what you were looking for. And two, Marscel had a million other things in his life—his law practice, his clients, Claudine. I don't. This search has my entire attention. All my resources, mental and physical, are dedicated to finding *The Key*."

"What if it's been destroyed? What if it never existed in the first place?"

"Unless we search, we'll never know. Tonight, we can get together somewhere quiet. You can relax and remember. Follow the charted rhythms of your heart."

"And what is that supposed to mean?" She gave a short laugh. "Charted rhythms of the heart sounds like an EKG."

"It means that your father cared deeply for you."

"Does it?"

When she met Flynn's gaze, her heart did seem to beat at a different rhythm, an uncomfortable, fast-paced rate that pulsed from her fingertips and centered below her ribcage. Either she needed a cardiogram or she was falling prey to his magnetism.

Effortlessly he'd enchanted Gretchen. And Claudine. And probably any other woman who caught his fancy. This beguiling man was hazardous to her self-control.

"Mollie? Will you meet with me tonight?"

"Sorry, I have a previous engagement."

Flynn gave a frustrated snort. She was still throwing up barriers. How could a lady who looked so complacent be so contrary? Stubborn, he thought. A spoiled brat. He watched as she folded her arms beneath the curve of her breasts. Her jaw thrust forward at a determined angle. And yet, strangely, he perceived a feminine welcome in her stance.

He wasn't imagining it. Flynn had enough experience with women to know when they *really* meant no, and Mollie's body language was saying yes. Her willingness was subtle—something in the way she cocked her hip. The hint of vulnerability when the wind off the lake teased her hair into soft brown waves. And her eyes. A man could drown in those eyes.

"Cancel your date tonight," he said.

"No. Perhaps, tomorrow."

"Listen, Mollie, I don't have a lot of time to waltz around with you. I've accepted an advance for the biography, and I've hinted that there might be a missing manuscript. My publishers want to see some words on the page."

"That's your problem. Not mine."

"Is it? Mollie, he wrote those words for you."

Though she avoided his gaze, he glimpsed a depth of emotion beneath her rigid facade. He sensed that she wasn't playing the tease, wasn't leading him on. There was something else. A secret? "You're the daughter of Woodrow Locke. His only child. You have much to contribute to our understanding of the man, of his genius. Yet, you've always held back. Why?"

"I don't know."

"What's so damn frightening?"

"I'm not scared."

"Why won't you talk about him?"

"Because I didn't know he was a genius. I was only a kid." Her eyes blazed. Her entire body was tense. "All I knew was that my father was a macho, paranoid, womanizing, alcoholic son of a bitch."

3

HER HAND FLEW UP to cover her mouth. But the words had already been spoken. No matter what she did, Mollie couldn't reclaim them. Her statement took on a life of its own, as huge and horrifying as a flame-breathing dragon.

Twelve years of "no comment" silence rose up to mock her. She'd maintained control and then—when she finally blurted—she'd chosen the worst possible confidante. Flynn was her father's biographer, the person who was dedicated to digging out dirty secrets and displaying them under chapter headings. Her privacy meant nothing to him; he only wanted to use her.

Her strategic retreat down the concrete stairs was halted by his hand on her shoulder. "Don't run away from me, Mollie."

Tension radiated from his touch, unbearably hot beneath the July sun. "I'm not running."

"Maybe I can help you."

From two steps below him, she peered up. His blond hair glistened like a mane. Above him on its pedestal was the stone lion with the frozen snarl. "At least stick to the truth, Flynn. You want to find the manuscript, and you want to learn about my father. I seriously doubt that helping me is anywhere on your agenda."

"But we're looking for the same thing."

"No, we're not." Her angry confusion melded into the bustle of the city streets, and she wished she could vanish so easily. Drop from sight. Have her words consumed and erased. She didn't think of her father that way. She didn't think of him at all if she could help it.

"We're both looking for the truth, Mollie."

"Leave me alone."

She stalked to the curb, miraculously hailed a taxi and dived into the back seat. "Go," she gasped to the driver. "Straight up Michigan. Go. Fast."

Through the rear window, she watched Flynn. He didn't pursue her. Instead, he paused at curbside, hands in his pockets. She could have sworn that she saw a sadness in his eyes, but that was impossible from half a city block away. Not even Flynn's magnetism could reach her from that distance. She had left him behind.

Mollie sprawled in the rear of the cab. The windows were rolled up, but the air conditioning was largely in the imagination of the driver. She yanked off her white linen jacket. There was a smear of dirt on the left shoulder where she'd leaned against the lion's pedestal. What a fool she was to wear white in the city! Foolish. Stupid. Dumb. Why had she even begun to listen to Flynn? Her rote "no comment" was the most practical approach to life. No more risk taking, she thought. No more listening to reckless schemes. She leaned forward in the cab. "Union Station, please."

On her way home, riding the Burlington commuter train to the Naperville station, Mollie practiced breathing normally. By the time she climbed into her car and drove the familiar route to her town house, her pulse was as regular as a metronome.

Her telephone answering machine was blinking when she came through the door, but she didn't play back the messages. She didn't want to hear Flynn's demands or Claudine's sweet patois or Marscel's guilt-inducing encouragement. She called her office and told Gretchen she would not be in for the rest of the day.

"What about your messages?" Gretchen asked.

"I'll deal with them tomorrow."

Mollie hung up and stumbled into her bedroom. Normally she didn't approve of midafternoon naps, but today had not been normal. She peeled off her clothes and crawled under her patchwork quilt. Very soon she succumbed to a blissfully dreamless sleep where nothing could touch her.

Hours later, she awoke with a start. Through the window, she saw the fading light of sunset. Her bedside clock showed 6:38 p.m. She was late.

With great haste, Mollie showered, dressed and dashed to her car. Tonight she'd made plans to see a movie with a twelve-year-old girl named Liana who was part of the Outreach program, and Mollie had screwed up. Again. Why was she making all these dumb mistakes? She sped across town to a cheerful old two-story house with a wide veranda. When she bolted up the stairs and punched the doorbell, it was 7:09 p.m.

A plump woman materialized behind the screen door.

"Sorry I'm late, Mrs. Volker."

"Won't you come in." Mrs. Volker held the screen open. "I'm afraid you've missed the start of the movie. And Liana must be home by nine o'clock. It's a school night."

"No problem," came a little voice from behind her. Liana stepped around Mrs. Volker, her foster mother, and edged through the open door. "We can go to the library. Right, Mollie?"

"Sure."

"No-o-o problem," Liana repeated. "We'll do something real cultural and be back by nine."

Mollie exchanged a bemused glance with Mrs. Volker. "Or else we'll go to the mall."

After she and Liana settled into her car, Mollie asked, "So, what's it going to be? Culture or the mall?"

"You got any cash?"

"Ten bucks that I was going to spend on the movie."

"Mall," Liana said.

For a twelve-year-old, she was quite decisive. But Liana was accustomed to taking care of herself. She hadn't had much of a childhood. Like many of the kids in Outreach, Liana was a runaway with a history of parental abuse. She and Mollie had been matched up for the past three months and had been going on outings once or twice a week.

"How are things with the Volkers?" Mollie asked.

"They're really nice. They're nerds, but they're nice. And the other three kids at the house are okay."

"You seemed anxious to go out tonight."

"Sometimes I just need to get away." Liana turned her huge brown eyes on Mollie. "You think I should get another hole in my ear at the mall? I met this rad guy at school, and I want him to like me."

"Because of the number of holes in your ear?"

Liana considered for a moment. "You're right. That's kind of old-fashioned."

They rode in companionable silence. Mollie had learned that Liana didn't like small talk. This dark, skinny girl with the expressive brown eyes only spoke when she had something to say. Or when she wanted something.

Also, Liana did not like to be touched. No hugs, please. So it was a surprise when she tapped Mollie's shoulder in the mall parking lot and said, "You don't look good. Problems with your boyfriend?"

"I don't have a boyfriend."

But after she parked, Mollie checked her reflection in the rearview mirror. She wore no makeup and, in her rush to meet Liana, had thrown on her walking shorts and a sleeveless T-shirt. "You're right. I'm a mess. I took a little nap and overslept."

"A nap in the daytime?" Liana's mouth stretched into a frown. "That's not you."

"Oh, really?" What she didn't need was psychological analysis from a twelve-year-old. Mollie was supposed to be the adult here. "And what is me?"

"You're all business. Never been late before tonight."

"And how does that make you feel?"

"I like it. Means you're human."

While they browsed through the mall, Mollie wondered how to encourage more communication from Liana. That was, after all, her function as an Outreach counselor—to give the child a nonthreatening confidante outside the foster home.

In an earring boutique, Liana offered a comment. "I like going to the mall with you. Can we do it again next week?"

"I'm going to be on a business trip for the next two weeks. But after that, malls are fine."

"After that."

Before her eyes, Liana closed down. Great, Mollie thought. The kid was just beginning to trust her and she had to leave town. "Liana, I'm sorry."

"Hey, no prob. You got to take care of business."

After five more shops, Mollie still was unsure of how to proceed. She decided on ice cream—vanilla for herself and mint chocolate chip for Liana. Though it didn't make the hurt go away, ice cream was a great remedy for guilt.

While they sat, lapping at their cones, Mollie asked, "This guy you like, is he in any of your classes?"

Liana ignored her question and pointed to a book-store window that was filled with a pyramid display of *Gateway* by Woodrow Locke. "Hey, that guy's got the same last name as you."

Mollie suddenly felt cold. "He was my father."

"Awright! And he's famous." Liana bounced up to the window and read the promotional copy. "'A genius. A superstar.' And here's a picture. Not bad looking for an old dude.'"

Shivering, Mollie threw away her half-eaten ice-cream cone. Her throat was constricted, frozen. She was never going to be able to escape the legend—the macho, womanizing, paranoid, alcoholic son of a . . .

Her emotions raced toward an outburst, and Mollie forced herself to slow down. It definitely was not cool for a counselor to have a nervous breakdown.

"What was it like?" Liana asked, rejoining her on the bench. "Having a famous dad?"

Mollie inhaled deeply and exhaled. Her lungs weren't working properly. She was suffocating, slowly dying.

"Mollie? Are you okay?"

"Sure." Her nod was terse. "I'm fine."

"So? What was it like?"

"Fine. Just fine."

Liana took a lick of her green ice cream. "You're lying."

"It wasn't great, okay? He and my mother got divorced when I was seven. And he died when I was fifteen. I barely knew the man. Now, let's talk about you."

"Did he ever hit you?"

"No," Mollie quickly replied. "He used to throw things sometimes and he yelled a lot. But he didn't hit."

"Did he drink?"

"Oh, yes. In those bookstore articles, you can read that he was a legendary man's man. Two-fisted. That means he had a shot of whiskey in one fist and a beer in the other. At one time, that was considered manly and colorful."

"My daddy was a wino."

Thrusting her past away from her, Mollie reached toward Liana, wishing to share with her, to encourage her to keep talking. "Tell me about your father."

The girl scooted away from her on the bench. "What about your mom? Was she a drunk? Did she hit you?"

"She never beat me. Maybe she wanted to, but she sent me to boarding school instead." Mollie laughed too loudly at her poor joke. "Mom passed away when I was twenty-one."

"You're lucky," Liana said darkly. She too discarded her unfinished ice cream. "I wish my mom and dad were dead."

"You don't really," Mollie surprised herself by saying. "Not until you figure out how you feel about them. Not until you've said goodbye the way you want to say goodbye."

"How do you know?"

"I don't. And I'm not doing a very good job of being a friend to you. I'm talking about myself."

"You never said goodbye?"

"No, I didn't. And I can't forget him."

"You ought to do it, Mollie."

Liana was right. She ought to do it for herself. Search for *The Key*. Not because she felt guilty about Marscel. Or because a missing manuscript from the great Woodrow Locke was so important. She owed it to herself to find out what her father had written especially for her. Then, maybe, she could finally say goodbye.

"Are you scared?" Liana asked.

"You bet. Looking at my past is like pushing aside a rock to see what crawls out from underneath."

On the other hand, she had to deal with it. Deal with it, she thought, like a card game. That idea wasn't so bad. She had a terrific poker face. Besides, her childhood problems were trivial when compared to the kids at Outreach, kids like Liana. Mollie hadn't been raped or savagely beaten or thrown into the streets to fend for herself. Her parents had been wealthy; her homes had been beautiful.

Deal with it. In her mind, she turned over a card. The king of hearts. Flynn. The dashing treasure hunter. His involvement created a disturbing factor. He was too charming, the kind of man who seduced women without trying.

"It's real scary," she said.

"You can do it." Liana rose from the bench, neared Mollie and held out her arms. Quickly Mollie enfolded her in a hug. Small, skinny Liana imparted an amazing amount of warmth. Holding her, Mollie almost cried. This had been the longest conversation they'd ever had, and the most important. In some mysterious way they had connected. And Mollie knew what she had to do.

MOLLIE RETURNED LIANA to the Volker's home by nine o'clock and drove slowly back to her town house. She parked in her driveway, reached across the seat for her purse and the book she'd bought at the mall, then stepped out of the car.

Overhead was a full, golden moon, the sort of moon that made people do crazy things, like volunteering for a treasure hunt. As she crossed the lawn to her porch, she heard a soft baritone chuckle, then a whispered, "Mollie."

"Who's there?"

Flynn stepped into the porch light. "Don't ever join the CIA, lady. I've been following you since you left the house at four minutes till seven, and you didn't once notice."

"What a sick thing to do!" But she smiled and held up the book she'd purchased. "A novel of suspense by Flynn Carlson. I guess you know all about the CIA."

"Not really." He winced with a slight crinkle of distaste around his eyes and mouth. "If I were a real spy, I'd know the identity of the girl you were with tonight."

"Her name is Liana. She's in the Outreach program."

"Aha! That's the charity you could greatly help by finding *The Key*."

"Aha, yourself. You're changing the subject." Mollie stroked the spine of his book, savoring his embarrassment. Humility was certainly different for him. She teased, "I thought novelists wrote what they knew?"

"Or what they dream." With one long-legged stride, he ascended the two concrete steps. Her porch, enclosed by a wrought-iron railing, was tiny, and he stood close. "For example, the heroine in that book is tall, lean and has green eyes. I've never known a woman like that. Until now."

"But she's blond." Mollie pointed to the cover.

"You're very literal, aren't you?"

"I guess poetry in the soul is not a genetically inherited trait. My father had it all."

"I don't believe that."

Flynn was near enough to see the delicately etched laugh lines around her eyes and the sprinkle of freckles across her nose. She was lovely, he thought, even without makeup.

A clean, fresh scent emanated from her, creating a special sensual aura in the night. He wanted to kiss her. And more. He wanted to know every inch of Mollie's body, to caress the velvet skin of her arm.

He gripped the iron porch railing and leaned away from her, trying to forget for the moment that Mollie was a desirable woman. He needed her in a different way. He needed her mind, her memories.

"I made my decision," she said.

"Wait. Don't tell me yet."

He studied her expression, trying to perceive her answer before she spoke. Earlier he'd thought she was easy to read. But now? Her lips curved in a slight downward quirk. Her gaze was steadfast. Maybe he didn't want to know the answer. "Mollie, if you say no, I won't push. I won't talk about Marscel's wish to find *The Key*. Or the needs of my publishers. Or my own curiosity about this book."

"Thank you so much for not mentioning those things."

"I'll try to understand."

But, damn, he was becoming obsessed with her—irrational enough to tail her in his rental car. Yes, it was sick and juvenile. He had never been the sort of man who skulked around, watching and fantasizing about a woman. When her appointment turned out to be with Liana instead of a date with another man, he'd been moronically relieved.

"It's up to you," he said. "All I ask, if you decide not to come with me and search for *The Key*, is an introduction to your uncle in Colorado."

"Well, that's very noble of you, Flynn. But I've decided to cooperate. It's important to me to find the book. And to make peace with my past."

His craggy features took on an expression of delight that irrationally pleased her. Flynn looked years younger, almost boyish. But when he moved to embrace her, she knew those muscular arms belonged to an adult man, and she dodged out of reach.

"Let's get one thing clear," she said. "I'm not doing this because I'm attracted to you. Some women find adventurers appealing, but I don't. I can't think of anything more ridiculous than skydiving and sailing around the world on one's handcrafted boat and riding bareback on dolphins."

"Actually, it wasn't a dolphin." He grinned. "It was a shark."

"That's just what I mean. You must agree not to pull any of that sort of nonsense with me."

"Agreed. I won't pack my machete."

"And I'm also not impressed by this." She gestured with his book. "Believe me, I've known a lot of authors, and they're a self-important, self-indulgent lot."

"Again, I agree. Anything else?"

Mollie slid easily into her efficient businesswoman persona. "Your idea of starting with my uncle is excellent. Since my father wrote that letter to Marscel from Colorado, it's logical that he hid the manuscript there." She checked her watch. There were a number of arrangements to be made, but it wasn't an impossible task. "I'll make the plane reservations. Pick me up tomorrow at noon, and we'll get started."

"May I come inside and we'll discuss this further?"

"I don't think so. There's quite a lot to be done." Mollie counted the tasks on her fingers. "Packing. A telephone call to Uncle Russ. Rearranging my work schedule."

She hadn't taken a vacation in three years, and now she was planning to fly off at a moment's notice. Very uncharacteristic. Very intense, but she could deal with it. With any luck, she could find the manuscript over the weekend and have her life in order by next Monday.

"Mollie, it seems to me that we should start inside your head. Let's explore your memories before we take off for Colorado. You could free-associate. Maybe you can follow the charted rhythms of your heart without leaving home."

"I'm afraid that's impossible."

"What?"

Mollie hesitated. "There's a reason that I've never discussed my childhood with the press or for biographies."

"Many of your memories must be painful."

"That's not it." Taking a deep breath, she plowed ahead. "I guess, psychologically, when a person has a kind of traumatic or weird upbringing—like mine—they have a lot of defenses about it. Sometimes, they develop phobias. Or have nightmares. In extreme cases, they might even take on a different identity."

"What are you saying?" He grinned. "That you're not really Woodrow Locke's daughter? That you're an imposter?"

"I might as well be." She shrugged helplessly. "I blocked it out."

His indulgent smile disappeared. "You are the most infuriating woman I've ever met. One minute you're going to help. The next, you say you can't remember. Which is it?"

"I said that I wanted to cooperate. And I will. But my memory isn't one hundred percent. It's not like punching a replay button on a VCR."

"How complete is this block of yours?"

She closed her eyelids slowly. Her mind was an unfocused screen where shadows flitted against hazy landscapes. She opened her eyes again. "To be perfectly honest, Flynn, I remember almost nothing."

4

WHILE MOLLIE STARED through the porthole window on the one-o'clock DC-10 to Denver, she was aware that Flynn was watching her. She also couldn't miss the obvious fact that the college-age woman who sat next to Flynn was practically drooling on his sleeve. Or that the perky blond flight attendant had given Flynn an extra portion of peanuts with his in-flight beer.

His freshman English classes must be outrageous, she thought, as she imagined the adventurous writer, Professor Flynn Carlson, facing a roomful of slobbering young women. The poor things. Fools for love. Mollie had experienced only one lovesick crush during her life, and she wouldn't wish that agony on anybody. A sharp twinge behind her eyelids reminded her of the pain she'd felt when she left Sergei, the sexy Russian artist.

It was the year after her mother died, and Mollie had been trying to figure out what to do with the rest of her life. She'd settled in Manhattan and found a job as a receptionist at an art gallery. Almost immediately she was swept off her feet by Sergei. He was average height and very dark—black hair and deep brown eyes. Not at all like Flynn, who was blond haired with eyes of an almost transparent blue. The physical contrast between Sergei and Flynn pleased her since it emphasized that Dr. Carlson was not her type.

Nor was he passionate like Sergei, who had kissed her within moments after they'd met and bedded her in a week. Never again, Mollie thought. Blinded by lust, she'd rented a studio for him and they'd spent six tumultuous months together. She'd done everything for that man. Promoted his art, supported him, fed him and coddled him. Ultimately she'd found him in bed with one of his models.

After Sergei, she moved to Chicago and established her well-regulated life at Onadime Office Supply. She'd sworn that she would never again allow a man to use her. So? What was she doing with Flynn?

Outside the window, a panorama of fluffy white clouds carpeted the route to Denver, the starting point for their search. But this situation was different than embarking on a romantic quest. Though Flynn was blatantly using her to find *The Key*, he didn't pretend to love her. Their alliance was actually refreshing. A partnership without any silly emotional attachments.

She turned her head and smiled at him.

"Hypnosis," he said.

"I beg your pardon?"

"We could try hypnosis to jog your memory."

"Could we?" she archly questioned. There didn't really seem to be much "we" in that suggestion. "Listen up, Flynn. I got myself packed, arranged to be absent from work, made the plane reservations and contacted Uncle Russ so we could stay with him in Denver. I'm doing my bit on this treasure hunt."

"Absolutely. Your efficiency is mind-boggling."

"Therefore, I hope you'll understand when I say that I do not wish to waste time with mumbo jumbo like hypnosis."

"Come on, Mollie. Hypnosis isn't a parlor game anymore. Psychiatrists use the technique all the time."

"I don't need a shrink." She turned back to the window. End of discussion.

Though he shrugged and said nothing, Flynn considered her refusal to be debatable. If not a shrink, she needed something or someone. Her anxiety about her father was a clear and present problem for her, especially since her memory block made such a huge incongruity with her otherwise well-organized life. It didn't make sense. Mollie seemed more like the type who would keep carefully catalogued photo albums and scrapbooks.

"Besides, I already tried it," she mumbled, "and it didn't work."

"You already tried hypnosis?"

"No, I tried a shrink. He was morbid and boring, and he seemed to think it would take years to get to the root of what he called my neurosis."

"What kind of psychiatrist was he?"

"An expensive kind."

"But was he Freudian? Jungian? Did he have a specialty?"

"Yes, he dealt with crazy people." She pressed her back against the airplane wall. "What sort of specialist do you think I need?"

"May I be frank?"

"Of course, we're in this together."

"I've done exhaustive research on your father and probably know more about him than you do. However, we've reached a similar conclusion. You said he was a paranoid, womanizing—"

"I know what I said." Mollie checked the emergency exits on the plane. She had a sudden urge to bail out.

"Alcoholic is the important descriptive word," he said. "It's very likely that your father was an alcoholic."

She recalled Liana saying that her father was a wino. "But my father was not a gutter drunk. His drinking was considered to have heroic proportions."

"That was true of many artists and writers during that era. Heavy drinking seemed to go hand in hand with spectacular prose." Flynn repositioned his long legs in the cramped airline space and raised his beer in an ironic toast. "Here's to them. The drinkers, the scoundrels and the writers. I only wonder how much more brilliant they would have been if they hadn't pickled their brains in alcohol."

"You're rather colorful yourself, Flynn."

The young lady seated to his right thought so, too. When she asked if he was a writer and Flynn responded, Mollie took the opportunity to slip out of their conversation and continue her morose observation of cloud patterns.

Even if her father had been an alcoholic, it didn't mean that Mollie needed a shrink. Though she occasionally sipped wine or beer, she couldn't possibly be called an alcoholic. More of a teetotaler.

After they'd landed in Denver, picked up a rental car and were en route to Uncle Russ's house, Flynn reintroduced the subject. "If your father was an alcoholic, there had to be an impact on you, Mollie."

"I have never had a drinking problem." Mollie was behind the wheel of the rental car, following the signs that led away from Stapleton airport. "I can count on one hand the number of times I've been even slightly tipsy."

"The behavior of an alcoholic affects his family."

"I know, I know. It's called codependence. In my work with the Outreach program, we've had a couple of lectures on it. Codependent children tend to form consuming attachments to others, usually other alcoholics or helpless people they can take care of. They suppress their own needs in favor of the addict. At the same time, they are fearful of intimacy, because if they trust someone, they are certain to be hurt."

"You forgot denial," he said.

"Denial means that the codependent will cover up to protect the physical addict. A codependent will deny the problem and will deny that it affects them. But there is usually some obvious betraying behavior." She thought of Liana. "Like refusing to be touched. Or never talking about themselves."

"Or a massive memory block."

"Really." Mollie could feel her temperature rising but kept herself in tight control. There were limits to how far she would allow Flynn to use her. "And what makes you such an expert?"

"I'm not an expert, but I've studied the subject."

"Denial is a catch-22," she said dismissively. "If I don't deny, then I acknowledge that I am codependent. But if I deny, that's a symptom of codependency. Sounds like a psychological trap, doesn't it?"

"Yes, it does."

"I prefer to look at the big picture. I'm competent, capable and have no relationships with addicts, as far as I know. There's nothing wrong with my mental health."

"Fine." To her relief, he dropped the subject. "Tell me what to expect from your Uncle Russ."

"He was eight years younger than my father and completely different from him. Uncle Russ was a successful attorney. He is now retired. He had three children and remained married to the same woman forever. When my grandparents died, he stayed here in Denver and took over the family home."

"Why is he opposed to giving interviews about your father?"

"I don't know. There was always a lot of competition between the two brothers. My father was better with a rifle. Uncle Russ was unbelievable with a bow and arrow."

"Do you think he resented your father's fame?"

"Maybe. Ask him."

"You're right." He mentally slotted those questions for the appropriate moment. "Let's talk about you, Mollie. What's it like for you to be back in Denver? I know that your family frequently visited for Christmas and summer vacations. Do these streets spark any memories?"

"Not really. I haven't been here since I was twelve."

"Think about it. Maybe you'll come up with some useful associations."

In the distance, she saw the Rocky Mountains west of town. Big and blue and beautiful. In the winter, snow would color the mountain white, glacial and secretive.

When she turned off the busy road, following the directions Uncle Russ had recited over the telephone last night, Mollie began to recognize her surroundings. Flynn was right; she felt old memories stirring.

"There's a park at the end of this road," she said. "My cousins and I used to go sledding there. It's beautiful in Denver after a snowfall. The ground is glittering and white while the skies are a dream of endless blue."

She remembered a trip into the mountains to chop down the family Christmas tree, then decorating the tree with special homemade ornaments, sipping eggnog and singing carols around the spinet.

"Christmas," she said, pleased to produce a completely average bit of nostalgia. "Santa Claus and carols and presents under the tree."

"Anything else?" he queried. "Any other memories?"

"Sorry, Flynn, no major clues." She added sarcastically, "I didn't suddenly recall that on my tenth Christmas my father presented me with an unpublished manuscript wrapped up with a big red bow."

"Just checking."

"I know and I don't mean to be snappish. But please don't analyze every word I say."

"How will I learn if I don't pay attention?"

"Listening is one thing," she said. "But I don't want to feel like you're footnoting and filing my every utterance. It reminds me of the media and those intellectual idiots who think they have the right to ask dumb questions."

"Like what?"

"Tell me, Miss Locke." Her impersonation took on a nasal, whining tone. "Did your father eat venison when he was writing his book about the elk? Was he constipated? Did he use a ballpoint pen or an ink pen? Did he have an affair with any famous poetesses? Artists? Movie stars?"

Flynn chuckled. "I'll try not to be like that."

"You're not," she assured him. "Plus, though there are limits to my cooperation, if it means we'll find *The Key*, I'm willing to be an amoeba under your microscope."

His gaze roamed over her body in a leisurely but not casual way. "You're much too shapely to qualify as a one-celled organism."

"Not to mention that I'm much too tall."

"I like tall women. They generally have terrific legs."

"You're a leg man, eh?"

"Don't get me started, Mollie. I'm trying my best to keep my analysis confined to your words and not your body."

"Good," she said quickly. "Because my body is definitely not part of our arrangement. Trust me, I don't have a treasure map tattooed on my—"

"Don't even say it." He gave an exaggerated groan. "I don't want to imagine tattoos."

Though their exchange had been lighthearted, Mollie was relieved when she parked on the street in front of the big old house that had belonged to her grandparents. Discussion of body parts did not belong in her relationship with Flynn. Not at all. She didn't want him thinking about her. Nor would she allow herself to visualize him as a man.

Her Uncle Russ had been sitting on the porch. When he came swaggering down the neat sidewalk toward their car, Mollie's heart took a jolt. Uncle Russ had aged. He'd allowed his hair to grow longer. He looked like her father.

Mollie reprimanded herself. This was Uncle Russ. Not Woodrow Locke. Russel Locke was a devoted family man, unlike her father. It was Uncle Russ who patiently taught Mollie to ride her first bicycle many Christmases ago.

He wrapped her in a bear hug and Mollie winced. He even smelled like her father. Stale cigars and whiskey on his breath. He held her at arm's length and squinted to study her. "You're prettier than I remembered, Mollie. A real Locke beauty."

Though her uncle's obvious inebriation disturbed her, Mollie forced herself to smile cheerfully. "That's not what you used to say, Uncle Russ. You and Dad teased me about being so tall and called me the Locke Ness monster."

Behind him, on the sidewalk, her aunt appeared. She was a tiny, quiet woman—the opposite of Uncle Russ's barrel-chested boisterousness. Feeling somehow disconcerted, Mollie made the introductions. "Dr. Flynn Carlson, this is my Uncle Russ and my Auntie..." Mollie stammered. For the life of her, she couldn't recall her aunt's given name. She never thought of her aunt as a person in her own right—only as a part of her uncle's identity.

The petite woman shook hands with Flynn. "I'm Yvonne Locke. Pleased to meet you."

"Auntie Von." Mollie embraced her. "I'm so sorry about dropping in on you at such short notice."

"Nonsense, child. We're delighted to see you. This big house seems terribly empty at times. And we insist that you stay here while you're in Denver."

"Thank you. I don't expect we'll be here for more than a day or two."

"Mollie can stay as long as she wants," Uncle Russ boomed. He jabbed his thumb in Flynn's direction. "But he's not welcome if he starts asking too many biographer questions. Got it?"

Auntie Von propelled them toward the rear of the car and asked brightly, "Is your luggage in the trunk?"

"Did you hear me, Flynn?" Uncle Russ teetered back on his heels. "I don't want any of this nosy stuff."

"Yes, sir."

"Yes, you will ask questions?" Uncle Russ pondered. "Or yes, you won't?"

Mollie hated that her uncle was drunk. If she had one ounce of gumption, she'd climb back into the car and drive away. She hated herself for not confronting him, for taking it. But she didn't leave. Instead, she chatted vivaciously while she unlocked the trunk of the car. Words tumbled into giggles and more words. Mollie had no idea of what she was saying, only that there was a need to fill the air, to chase away the demons, to kill the dragons.

When Auntie Von touched her arm, Mollie turned, wide-eyed. "Yes, Auntie? What is it?"

"He'll be all right, Mollie. Calm down."

"Of course. Sure, fine." Mollie backed away from the open trunk. She stumbled on the pavement, but righted herself. Breathing was difficult. Must be the high altitude.

"Here we go," Uncle Russ said. He lifted their suitcases from the trunk and set them cautiously on the pavement. With a glance at Flynn, he took Mollie's case—the larger and heavier of the two. "This way."

Uncle Russ lumbered up the sidewalk to the house, followed by Flynn, then Mollie and her aunt. When they entered the house, Mollie felt as though she'd stepped through a door into her past. All those Christmases with festive decorations and boughs of evergreen. And noise from a houseful of family. Her gaze absorbed the gleaming white walls, family photos, polished oak floors, the sweeping staircase to the second floor, and she half expected to see her grandparents, dressed like Mr. and Mrs. Santa Claus. Mistletoe had always been hung in the front foyer.

Mollie remembered her mother and father kissing while she sat on the stairs, quiet as a mouse, and watched. "It's good to be here. I've been away too long."

"I've assigned you to your old bedroom upstairs. And Dr. Carlson is down the hall." Auntie Von looked up, momentarily confused. "Unless you'd rather be in the same—"

"They wouldn't," Uncle Russ said. "Not under my roof. Not with some damn writer." He dropped Mollie's suitcase in the front foyer and glared at Flynn. "Ever shoot a bow and arrow?"

"Yes, sir, I have."

Uncle Russ thrust out his chin. His arms dangled loosely at his sides, fingers twitching. Mollie recognized the attitude. She'd seen her father assume that pose dozens of times. Generally it was right before he made a scene.

Frantically she tried to divert her uncle's attention. "You look terrific, Uncle Russ. Have you been working out? Jogging?"

Uncle Russ ignored her. "Let's see how good a shot you are, Flynn. You come with me into the backyard, pal."

"Russel," Auntie Von snapped. "I think Mollie and Dr. Carlson might be tired. Let's allow them to get settled."

Uncle Russ swung around to stare at Flynn. "Do you need a nappy-poo? Or you want to show me what you're made of?"

Flynn dropped his suitcase in the foyer. "Let's go, Russ."

When the two men stormed toward the rear of the house, Mollie turned helplessly to her aunt. "What's gotten into Uncle Russ?"

"Your uncle is an alcoholic."

"Not really," Mollie quickly defended. "I mean, I know he's been drinking, but . . ." It didn't seem possible. Mollie didn't remember him that way at all. He'd been normal, a good father to her cousins. Gruff, but kindhearted.

"He's been in Alcoholics Anonymous for ten years," Auntie Von said, "but he occasionally falls off the wagon. Today is one of those occasions."

"Oh, Auntie Von, I'm so sorry. I had no idea."

"Surely you remember those Christmases when the menu ranged from wine to alcoholic eggnog to hot-buttered rum."

"I never noticed."

"Of course not, and I'm not accusing you. How could you remember? You were only a child."

But she wasn't blind or deaf. Mollie had treasured those snowy Christmases. How could she have been so unfeeling?

"It's a disease, Mollie. Your father wasn't the only one who succumbed to it." Auntie Von nodded sadly. "Now, we'd better go outside and watch your uncle make an ass of himself."

"Isn't there something we can do?"

"Russ has to do it for himself. One day at a time. In this case, it's more like one hour at a time. But I think he's just about played out."

Mollie couldn't decide which was stranger. Uncle Russ being an alcoholic, or Auntie Von putting up with him for all these years. A disease, huh? She'd heard that line before during her training as an Outreach counselor, but she couldn't quite accept it. If Uncle Russ had cancer, he would have told her. The whole family would have gathered around to support him. This was different.

On the back lawn were three large bull's-eyes, backed with bales of hay. Uncle Russ had provided Flynn and himself with handsome wooden bows.

"I'll go first," Uncle Russ announced. "So Flynn here can see how it's done."

His loose-limbed clumsiness vanished the instant he notched his arrow in the taut-stringed bow. Again Mollie's breath caught in her throat. He was so like her father—weaving and drunk, yet somehow magnificent.

He let the arrow fly. It struck near the center of the target. "Not bad for an old duffer. Eh, Mollie? Now let's see if your young man can compete."

"He's not my young man," she muttered.

But when Flynn took a wide-legged archer's stance, she found herself cheering in her heart. She wanted him to be a hero, wanted him to win, to beat the pants off this vicious old man who masqueraded as her kindly Uncle Russ.

And Flynn certainly looked as if he knew what he was doing. The muscles in his forearm tightened as he gripped the polished bow and tugged the bowstring back. Squinting beneath his eyebrows, he took careful aim. Then he let the arrow fly.

When it hit the outer edge of the target, Uncle Russ hooted, "Is that the best you can do?"

"It sure as hell isn't."

Flynn notched another arrow and released. Then another. Two bull's-eyes.

Uncle Russ gaped at the target, then stared at Flynn. "I guess you pass the test." In a lightning change of mood, he slapped Flynn on the shoulder. "Okay, buddy, ask your questions. You're the man to write my brother's story."

"*The Key,*" Flynn said. "What do you know about it?"

"It was a book Woody wrote for Mollie. Never published the thing. He wanted to give it to her when she was old enough to understand. It might even be stashed around here someplace."

A small cry escaped Mollie's lips. It did exist. *The Key* was a reality.

5

UNCLE RUSS SANK DOWN onto a lawn chair, frowning at his bow as if it had betrayed him. "I don't know where it is. Not for certain."

"*The Key?*" Flynn probed.

"That's what we were talking about. Pay attention."

"Tell me everything you remember about *The Key*." Flynn sat beside him. "Did you read the manuscript?"

"Why in the heck would I—"

Auntie Von interrupted. "I have a better idea, Dr. Carlson. You and Mollie could search the attic of this house. We've been accumulating bits and pieces up there for fifty years."

"Great!" Mollie waved to Flynn. "Let's go."

Flynn nodded to Uncle Russ. "We'll talk later."

Auntie Von led them through the house. In a brief detour, they dropped off their suitcases in their second-floor rooms, then proceeded through a door and up a narrow staircase. Mollie felt like Alice venturing into the rabbit hole. The attic was new to her. Though she'd spent considerable time in this house, she'd never explored this mysterious place before. A sense of anticipation bubbled through her. *The Key* must be here; she felt unspoken words from her father drawing her. What a lucky twist of fate that her family had lived in this house forever! Decades of Locke history had remained intact.

Two bare bulbs and sunlight from dormer vents illuminated the attic that stretched from one end of the house to the other. The dry hot air trapped dust motes in a musty haze. The walls, covered with pink insulation material, sloped sharply on either side. Much of the space on the rough wood floor was cluttered, but part of the attic was neatly arranged with metal shelving.

"Those shelves were where I tried to get organized," Auntie Von said. "I must've thrown away two dozen boxes of mildewed clothes and old papers."

"Papers?" Flynn asked.

"School assignments and artwork from the grand-children. Most things with Woody's name on them, I packed up and sent to Marscel. Except for what's in here." She tapped a cardboard box labeled "Woody." "There are several manuscripts in here, but they're all scribbled on." She gestured to the rest of the attic. "Who knows what you'll find in the rest of this junk."

With that benediction, she left them.

Mollie spread her arms wide, gathering the sticky atmosphere like a bouquet of roses. "This is wonderful, Flynn. We're going to find *The Key* today."

"You're sure?"

"It's perfect! We started at the most logical point and came to the most direct conclusion. Organized thinking pays off. Ta-da!" Her laughter echoed in the attic. She thumped out a happy victory dance on the dusty wooden floor and flung herself into Flynn's arms. "We've done it!"

Her impulsive embrace took Flynn by surprise . . . for about two seconds. Then he instinctively responded to her soft female body. He wrapped his arms around her, held her close. Her hair brushed like a silk scarf on his cheek. Her breasts crushed against his chest. He could feel her breath, her heartbeat.

"Oh, lady, you don't know what you're doing to me." He fought his sexual attraction to her, but it only took one innocent hug to arouse him.

Mollie immediately wriggled out of his arms. "I'm sorry if I gave you the wrong impression."

"Mollie, I didn't mean . . ." He took a step toward her, then stopped. With a stiff jolt of willpower, he brought himself under control.

"I'm sorry about Uncle Russ," she said, then quickly changed the subject. "Where'd you learn archery?"

"On the farm when I was growing up." Flynn sighed, resigning himself to her inaccessibility. Her wide green eyes were frightened as a deer facing a wolf in the forest. "Did your uncle's drunken behavior waken any memories for you?"

"Let's not talk about that now."

"When, Mollie?"

Flynn had purposefully posed a double-edged question. When would she start remembering? When would she stop avoiding contact with him? Her answer told him that she understood both meanings. "When I'm ready."

She turned away from Flynn, hands on hips, and stalked across the attic floor. Mollie cursed herself for mindlessly leaping at him. She didn't want to start anything sexual with Flynn. Yet the imprint of his body left a lingering impression. His scent clung to her. She could still feel the strength in his arms when he'd embraced her.

The attic seemed hotter, nearly unbearable. "I guess we'd better get started," she said. "You take the box that Auntie Von has already sorted. I'll go through this other stuff."

While she buried herself in a mountain of junk, Flynn cracked open the cardboard box. The first layer was just old bills and scraps of nonsense. Then he hit pay dirt.

"My God, Mollie. These are first drafts with your father's corrections in his own handwriting."

Her head poked out from behind a standing lamp with a cracked shade. "So?"

"Not even Marscel has corrected drafts."

"So?"

"So this is a remarkable find for the biography. I'll be able to document his thinking and his imagery as no one has ever been able to do. This is like a map to his subconscious."

The white onionskin paper trembled in his hand, and Flynn realized he'd been holding it so tightly he'd nearly ripped an edge. This was the break he needed. His New York publishers had been pressuring him to come up with something, and the only progress Flynn had offered was the possibility of an unpublished Locke manuscript.

The Key had kept them satisfied for a while. But Flynn had blown every deadline for submission of a completed proposal, and his editor was dropping dire hints. If Flynn couldn't furnish a biography while Woodrow Locke was still hot news, the assignment might fall to someone else. Someone like Edleman, that pugnacious jerk at the banquet.

These scribbled papers made all the difference.

Flynn carefully shuffled deeper. There were chapters so thick with corrections that they were unreadable. And poems. Some of the poems had sketches and doodling along the margins. Several repeated a similar pattern. Hatch marks like tick-tack-toe with squiggles in the middle. Flynn carried one scrap through the attic clutter and showed it to Mollie. "Do you know what this scribbling means?"

She looked up from the steamer trunk she'd been digging through. "It looks like a graph."

"Or a map?"

Mollie sat back on her heels and wiped the sweat from her forehead. "You don't really think we'll find a map up here with an X marks the spot?"

"Stranger things have happened."

When their eyes met, Mollie quickly looked away. Stranger things, eh? Like being attracted to a man who was using her? Partly to ward off his spell, she held up a small redwood box. "Look what I found. My all-time favorite Christmas present."

She carefully lifted the lid, revealing a plastic ballerina who pirouetted in circles on a mirror. A tinkling version of "Moonlight Sonata" accompanied the dance. "Grandma Locke gave it to me."

"Do you remember the day?" he asked.

"December twenty-fifth, of course. I was seven." She paused. "Maybe I was six. I'd just lost a tooth."

"That's pretty good remembering," he said.

"But it's just a music box. Nothing significant."

"We don't have many paths into your memory. Give yourself a chance to follow this one." He stood and started back across the attic. "Close your eyes and think about it. I'll be over here with the scribblings."

"Think about the music box," she mumbled. That suggestion was almost as dumb as hypnosis. Especially now when it looked as though they would find *The Key* without having to probe Mollie's memories at all. Purposely she set the music box aside. The manuscript must be here. Why bother with memories?

After several hot, grueling hours, Mollie finished digging through the mess on the far side of the attic. Though she'd unearthed a lace shawl, tons of hardback books and a number of damaged dolls, she'd found nothing that resembled a manuscript.

Much later that evening, after dinner with Auntie Von and a good-night to Flynn, who had dragged the cardboard box full of Locke's papers down to his bedroom, Mollie picked up the redwood music box again.

Dressed in her cotton nightgown, she stretched across the double bed in the room where she'd slept as a child. "Moonlight Sonata." Such lovely, gentle music. In the instant before she lifted the redwood lid, another tune flitted through her mind. A nameless little song. She paused to listen, but it was gone.

Mollie stroked the polished redwood, and watched the ballerina spinning endlessly. A pleasant memory. She closed her eyes and visualized herself as a girl, lying on the soft double bed she'd shared with her cousin, Diane, at Christmastime. She imagined huge snowflakes drifting silently through the glow of the street lamp outside the bedroom window. The tinkling music had a mesmerizing effect on her. The gentle serenade filtered through her mind, blanking everything else.

Then there were other sounds. Less Christmasy noises. The sharp tones of adult voices from down the hall. She heard the low rumble of her father's voice and her mother's sharp retorts. The words were unclear, but the emotion came through. Her parents were arguing. There was a loud crash.

Mollie saw herself as a child, pulling the box closer, hoping to drown out anger with "Moonlight Sonata." Her adult hands mimicked the child as she stroked the shiny wood surface of her music box. If only she could be a beautiful ballerina, swirling in endless circles on a mirror.

A single tear rolled down her cheek. She snapped closed the box and the voices in her head went quiet. Silence was better. When she slept, she did not dream.

THE NEXT MORNING, Mollie found Flynn and her uncle sitting over coffee. Though Uncle Russ looked at her through rheumy, bloodshot eyes, he wasn't drunk.

A sprawl of encyclopedias and atlases blanketed the kitchen table. Flynn dug underneath one and produced a sheet of onionskin paper. "I found this last night, Mollie. What do you make of it?"

She held the paper by its edges. Another graphlike scribble with a skinny blob in the middle. Two words were written across the top: *The Key.*

"It's got to be a map," Uncle Russ said. "Woody was fascinated by maps, longitude and latitude."

Mollie nodded. Again, that odd, nameless tune, the one she'd vaguely remembered last night, danced through her mind. "Is this an island in the middle?"

"That's what we thought," Flynn said, gesturing to the books. "And we figured it might be in the Florida Keys, because your father spent a lot of time there. But the shape doesn't match anything."

"It's long," she said. "Like a peninsula?"

"Possibly. But there are these other lines beside it. As if this piece in the center were separate from a mainland."

She shrugged. "I don't know."

"Nor do I." Auntie Von bustled from the kitchen with a fresh pot of coffee and a mug for Mollie. "But Russ did have an idea that you could work on today. Up in the mountains."

"Right," Uncle Russ said. "There was a cabin where we stayed when we went fishing on the Platte."

"Of course, that was only a rental," Auntie Von said. "But there was some hiding place that you kids had up there."

Without consciously remembering, Mollie replied, "A cave."

"The ideal hiding place for buried treasure," Flynn mused.

"As a matter of fact," Mollie said. "It's a terrific hiding place."

As soon as Mollie finished her coffee, Auntie Von shooed them out the door. Headed west in the rental car with Flynn driving, Mollie read the directions that Uncle Russ had written out for them. "I think we take the Morrison turnoff."

"But of course, you don't remember."

"How could I? The last time we took a family fishing trip, I was only ten or eleven years old."

"In other ways, is your memory block still complete?"

"Certainly."

Her response negated last night's experience with the music box, but Mollie wasn't quite ready to talk about that yet. The threatening rumble of her father's voice in argument with her mother was the clearest recollection she'd ever had. Almost real. As if he weren't dead. As if he hovered behind her shoulder, waiting for her to turn around and recognize him.

Mollie blinked him away. She wanted to read *The Key*, to see his special message to her. Perhaps then she would be willing to turn around and face him.

For now she was content to feel the city fading behind them as they entered the arid foothills. Sweeping vistas of scrubby pine and rugged hills gave reality to their search. They were looking for words on pages, not memories.

"Does anything look familiar?" Flynn asked.

"A mountain is a mountain is a mountain." She stuck her arms out the open car window to feel the breeze. "And isn't that a Gertrude Steinish observation? Maybe my father hung out with her, too."

"She was a bit before his time."

Flynn seemed tense, and she wondered if he was upset about not finding the manuscript in the attic. "Is something wrong?"

"Yes."

"Would you like to tell me about it?"

"Okay, Mollie, here it is. I'm beginning to rethink the viability of this entire quest. I talked with my publishers this morning, and they aren't as thrilled about the discovery of your father's first drafts as I am. They want *The Key*."

"We'll find it."

"I don't think so, Mollie. Frankly, I was counting on your memories to track down the possible locations. Even after you told me that you'd blocked out great chunks of your past, I thought we could break through. But after this morning, I finally understand why you're not going to remember. Not now. Probably, not ever."

She didn't recall anything unusual about this morning. She had coffee, exchanged small talk and they'd left. "What are you referring to?"

"At breakfast this morning, there seemed to be a case of collective amnesia. Yesterday, your uncle was drunk and obnoxious. Today at the kitchen table, you all acted as if nothing happened."

"Well, what's the point in an apology? Of course, he's sorry. And, of course, we forgive him."

"Forgive and forget," Flynn said. "Don't you see, Mollie? You were trained to forget what happened to you. That's not going to change."

"I'm willing to try."

"Okay. Then let's make an aggressive attempt."

She nodded.

"I'll start feeding you clues. I know a hell of a lot about your father from my studies. I'll talk, and you tell me if anything strikes a chord."

Mollie stared through the window at the winding two-lane byway. Through the pines, she spied the sparkling reflection of a tiny stream at roadside. Flynn's idea sounded dangerous to her, a venture into uncharted territory.

"Here's where you turn," she said. "According to Uncle Russ's directions, the cabin is straight down this road. But go to the left. When the dirt road ends, we'll have to walk the rest of the way to the cave."

"You remembered that all by yourself," he pointed out. "Your uncle didn't know the location of the cave."

"Okay, Flynn. Since you're so set on this plan, I'm willing to try. Feed me a memory."

He dug into his shirt pocket and pulled out the onion-skin paper with the scribbled map. "Concentrate on this."

Turning the paper one way, then another, it was still an indecipherable blob. "I have no idea what this is supposed to represent. I might be able to give you the location if this map had longitude and latitude markings." As she spoke, that odd tune bounced in her head again. She hummed it. "I keep thinking of this song. Do you know it?"

He listened carefully. "It doesn't sound familiar. But repeat it. We'll both remember it."

Humming the song for him produced a strange sense of intimacy. She recited the notes. He repeated. Then, again. It was as if she were giving away part of herself.

And Mollie wasn't totally comfortable with that particular kind of sharing. She didn't really trust Flynn, didn't know him. "I think you've misjudged the situation. I'm sure that my memories won't have anything to do with finding *The Key*."

"What about the key to yourself?" he reminded her. "Making peace with your past. That was the reason you decided to come on this search."

"Aren't you clever to remember that." She gritted her teeth. "All right. Let's talk memories."

"We'll take something obvious. Your father's work habits. No matter how late he'd been out on the night before, he always rose with the sun and went to his desk to start writing."

"If you say so."

"Do you remember his desk?"

"No. I've seen pictures of him sitting at a desk."

"Think of those pictures," Flynn encouraged in a gentle voice. "Your father would write in the early morning hours. At his desk."

"And he kept his booze in the bottom left drawer."

A hazy picture formed in the back of her mind. Her father. His desk. She hated his desk because when he was there he was too busy to spend time with her.

"He wrote in longhand," Flynn cued her. "Then he would type the first draft. Imagine the sound of his typing."

She tried, but all she could hear was the sound of gravel crunching beneath their tires.

"He kept the typed pages in a wooden box," Flynn said. "Are you getting anything, Mollie?"

"When he was done," she said, "he'd take off his reading glasses, rub his eyes. And the bottom left drawer would open." Pain, sharp as a cleaver, chopped off her remembrance. "Sorry. I don't remember anything else."

"It's a start."

"There's something else. A clock? No, something else that ticks." She felt as if she were poised at the edge of discovery. The actual memory was one step farther. One pace closer to the brink. She could almost touch it. The fog shrouding her mind thinned to a shimmering mist. Memories began to emerge as misshapen lumps. In panic, Mollie retreated. "I don't know."

"Tell me, Mollie. Try to tell me."

She could hear the ticktock getting louder. But it was a happy sound, nothing to be afraid of. She heard her father's laughter. Then it was gone.

They had reached the end of the road leading to the cave. "We're here." Mollie swallowed hard. "I'll have to concentrate on it later."

Flynn watched as her emotional shield slid back into place. For a moment, he'd thought she would remember. Her green eyes had softened. Her lips had parted as if the words would tumble from her. Then, purposefully, she'd closed off.

Though this was only the second day of their quest, his frustration level had hit an all-time high. Her memories had to be a valuable storehouse of information, but he couldn't unlock the doors. Why, dammit? Her past couldn't have been all bad. There must have been good times. Why was she so afraid?

He climbed out of the car and joined her beside the tiny stream.

"You're angry," she said.

"It's not your fault, Mollie. I'm not the most patient man in the world. When I want something, I go after it.

But I can't grab you and shake this information out your ears."

"I'm not trying to be difficult."

"Then do it. Take the step backward into your memories. No matter what you find, I'll be here for you."

"Until the manuscript is found," she clarified. "Then, it will be 'Farewell, Flynn.' You'll be on to other challenges."

"If you need me, I'll stay with you."

"Caring for poor Mollie? The emotional cripple? No, thank you. I don't want pity, damn you."

"Damn me all you want. But don't damn yourself. It's your past. Go ahead and experience it. Be angry. Be hurt. Go ahead and feel sorry for yourself. You have reason. Your parents went through a bloody divorce. Your father was a heavy drinker. He died young. But there has to be something good, too."

His simplification infuriated her. "So, you think it's a matter of looking past the thorns to see the roses."

"In a way. Everybody had problems in their childhood. Move past them, Mollie. You can do it."

"Just like that, huh? Snap my fingers and move right on." She stared up at him. "Don't you get it? That's exactly what I have done. I didn't think about it. I try to forget that I'm Woodrow Locke's daughter. Until you came along with your stupid treasure hunt, I was doing fine."

"Except for a lack of personal relationships. And anxiety attacks."

"Leave me alone." Angrily she whirled away from him toward the forest.

Instantly Flynn reacted. His hand shot out and caught her arm. His jaw tensed. Cold fury turned his blue eyes to ice.

She could see him struggling for control. When he spoke, his voice was dangerously calm. "I will not leave you alone, Mollie. I'm going to be here, reminding you; pushing you. Until you find what you're looking for."

"Let go of my arm."

"With pleasure."

His iron grip loosened and she pulled away from him. With deliberate strides, her long legs carried her along a forest path. In a quaking stand of green-leaved aspen, she paused and stared dry-eyed at the wooded hillsides around her. The arid scent of earth tingled in her nostrils with each deep breath that she took.

She should quit right now before she completely lost control of her life. Give up, she told herself. So what if her father wrote a book for her? She needed to put miles between Flynn and herself, wanted to return to her calm life. But Mollie knew she wouldn't. The commitment had been made, and she was a woman who honored her promises.

Damn Flynn. She wouldn't give him the satisfaction of quitting. She'd remember. She'd find *The Key*.

6

WHILE HE TRAILED BEHIND HER, Flynn stared down at the path or far into the distance or skyward or backward or anywhere but at Mollie. Her athletic stride in her snug blue jeans was painfully distracting. It was obvious that the woman despised him. He must be crazy to still find her desirable. She was frustrating, difficult and stubborn. He didn't want to care. More specifically, he didn't want to be aroused by her.

Her assessment of their relationship had been accurate. They would find the manuscript, then he'd be gone, off to other challenges. Was that unfair? He hadn't promised more. Nor had she. In fact, when he got right down to the bottom line, he wondered who was using whom.

All along, he'd suspected that Mollie was a tease, offering delectable promises and then darting away. She was like a green-eyed mermaid who enchanted seamen with her beautiful song until the poor fools lost their bearings and crashed on a coral reef. Not this sailor, he decided. No matter what she did, no matter how much he wanted her, Flynn vowed to stay afloat.

He watched her hiking before him with straight shoulders and long legs. He could watch her without falling apart. So what if she appealed to him? Then Mollie turned and faced him with glittering eyes and a slight sad pull to her mouth. The chemistry he felt inside made a mockery of his logical vows.

"I'm sorry," she said. "I shouldn't have snapped at you."

"Apology accepted." He closed the scant distance between them. "And I shouldn't have pushed you so hard."

"Maybe not." She scrambled down the path into a cosy green glen beside the stream and perched on a flat gray rock. "We're not going to find *The Key* in Denver. It wasn't in the attic, and I can't imagine that it would go unnoticed anywhere else in the house. I hate to admit it, but you were right, Flynn. The best clues are probably stashed away inside my head."

He sat on a rock opposite her, trying not to notice the dappled sunlight playing in her soft brown hair. "What about this cave?"

"Doubtful. I don't think my father even knew about the cave. It was a hideout for my cousins and me."

Flynn nodded his agreement. "I'm afraid you're right. I don't think we'll find the manuscript here. However, your father was unpredictable. Anything is possible."

With a shock, Flynn realized that he'd be damn sorry if they did find the manuscript in this cave. The discovery would mean that his time with Mollie was over. Their quest would be completed too soon, and he wasn't ready to let her go.

"This trip to Denver was a waste of time."

"Not at all." He pointed out the positives, "I found those remarkable first drafts. Your uncle corroborated the existence of *The Key*." He dug into his pocket and produced the piece of onionskin paper. "And we have this map."

Mollie took the map from him and studied it. "The shape doesn't match anything in the Keys?"

"Not really."

"What's another island that might be associated with my father? Hawaii? Japan?"

Flynn shook his head. "Your father spent most of his life in Colorado, Paris, the Keys and New York City."

Mollie positioned the map so the blob in the middle was almost vertical and turned it so Flynn could see. "Did you say New York City?"

"Manhattan." He sprawled backward on the rock and peered through pine boughs into the blue sky. "How could I have missed it? That island is Manhattan."

"Rather an impossible place to search." Mollie frowned. She hadn't been back to Manhattan since she and Sergei had split up, and she wasn't thrilled about following the charted rhythms of her heart to that particular city.

"Okay." Flynn sat up straight. "If we don't find anything in the cave, the next stop is New York. That's convenient for me because I need to visit with my editor, anyway. But you? Will you come with me, Mollie?"

Hauling herself upright, she dusted off the backside of her jeans. Manhattan? SoHo? The Village? Talk about marching into the jaws of painful memory. She stole a quick glance at Flynn. His eyebrows were raised in question. How could he look so innocent? If only she could trust him, this wouldn't be such a daunting task.

"If it's necessary," she said with a sigh, "I'll go to New York. Now, let's check out this cave."

She searched the trees and rocks for direction. It had been a long, long time since she'd been in this forest. With a wide leap, she crossed the trickling stream.

"Mollie, do you know where you're going?"

"I think so." She picked her way along the stream's edge, threading her way through a maze of trees. Finally she pointed. "That's the cave. Right in front of us."

A dark crevasse between giant boulders beckoned to her. She caressed the cold rugged stone and peered into the dark passageway between them. Oh, yes, she'd been here before. In a secret place where she felt safe.

She peeled off her socks and sneakers. "We have to wade through the stream to get there."

"Great. You know how cold that water is going to be?"

"Some adventurer you are," she teased. "After climbing Mount Everest, you're afraid to get your feet wet."

"I didn't climb Everest," he muttered. "Marscel had that wrong. It was Mount Rainier."

"Good. Because once we get behind these boulders, we have to scale a rock wall."

Rolling up the legs of her jeans, she stepped into the icy stream and gasped with delight. The sparkling water rushed over her feet and ankles. Carefully she picked her way along the streambed and entered a cathedral of boulders. Huge slabs of rock balanced in high, precarious spires, seemingly prepared to crash down at any moment. But Mollie recognized this place, and she knew these rocks had not changed their position during the years she'd been away.

Shafts of sunlight flowed through cracks between the rocks, reflecting brilliantly on a small pool. A rippling waterfall fed the pond, then descended in a rush toward the entryway.

"It's beautiful," Flynn's voice echoed.

But Mollie was already far ahead of him. She'd replaced her sneakers. With unerring instinct, she found handholds and tiny outcroppings for her feet as she scrambled up a rock wall. Conscious thought faded as she ascended to a jutting ledge.

Crawling on hands and knees, she entered the cave behind the ledge. It felt damp inside. And only large enough to hold secret meetings with her cousins. Her hand groped behind a loose rock and discovered the stub of a candle and a matchbox wrapped in plastic.

"I can't believe it," she whispered in amazement. "I can't believe it's still here."

She had changed since those childhood days when she and her cousins had discovered this burrow beyond the waterfall. Mollie was a grown woman with responsibilities, a different person. And yet the rocks had not shifted their form.

Outside, she heard Flynn cursing. "Mollie," he shouted. "Where are you?"

"Up here," she called, poking her head through the cave's entryway.

When he spied her, he spread his hands wide. "And how did you get up there?"

"I climbed. It's easy. Just take your time."

A ray of sunlight sparked gold highlights in his hair as he negotiated his way through the outer cavern. Mollie noticed that his pant legs were wet. At the rock wall, he had difficulty with the ascent that she'd climbed as easily as a ladder. A doubtful frown creased her forehead. Did she really want to invite Flynn into her cave? Her secret hiding place?

He climbed closer. His fingers, white knuckled, gripped tiny fissures in the rock as he slowly made his way nearer and nearer.

For a moment, Mollie considered deserting her cave, telling him truthfully that there was no clue to finding the missing manuscript within and that they might as well leave. His nearness threatened her, and she worried about exposing too much of her private self to a man who'd already admitted that he was using her.

But he was nearly at the ledge. "Give me a hand, Mollie."

"You're too heavy." She hesitated. "I can't pull you up."

Yet, when he slipped, she instinctively grasped his wrist to steady him. Using her as an anchor, Flynn completed the climb. He sprawled on the ledge beside her. "Gee, that was a whole bunch of fun."

"You're wet."

"I slipped in the stream," he admitted. "So I'm probably also black-and-blue."

"Too bad," she said nervously. "Because I just figured out that there isn't a single clue in this place."

"Probably not. I don't believe your father ever was here."

"Why not?"

"He would have written about it. I'm not in the same league with your father, but I am a writer, Mollie. And this place is spectacular. The way these rocks are thrown together. The waterfall. The light filtering down is magical as Merlin's cathedral. Beautiful. One of nature's metaphors. And I've found no such cave in any of your father's works."

"What about the unpublished manuscript we're searching for? What about *The Key*?"

Flynn shook his head. "This place is yours, Mollie. Not your father's. And I'm glad you brought me here."

She knew he was too close. The whisper of the waterfall surrounded them with frightening intimacy. "We'd better go."

"Will you show me the inside of your cave?"

Though she tried to remain nonchalant, Mollie knew that something unusual was happening to her. Not since childhood had she revealed so much of herself to another human being, but she didn't feel out of control. She knew that if she demanded that they turn back, Flynn would accept her decision. "Let me go first," she said. "It's dark in there."

Inside the cave, her fingers fumbled with the matches. Finally she sparked a small flame and lit the candle. "Okay, Flynn, you may come in."

When Flynn scrunched his tall frame through the entryway, Mollie was exploring the cave walls, holding the candle very near the rocky surface. "Here," she pointed. "I wrote my initials."

The candlelight flickered across her features, and Flynn was mesmerized by the mysterious reflection. Her hair had turned into a halo of wild curls from the moisture of the waterfall. Her green eyes were lit with an inner glow. Magical. He'd suspected that she was an enchantress, and now he was certain.

"See." She pointed again. "D.L. is Diane Locke, my cousin who's only one year younger than I am. She's been married three times. No children."

"A shame," Flynn said. "This cave should be a legacy passed on from generation to generation."

She sat cross-legged on the bedrock floor. "That's a wonderful thought. I'd like to pretend that the only people in the whole world who know about this cave are my cousins and me."

"And me," Flynn said.

"And you." But his presence seemed right. In this tiny cavern, Flynn was not a biographer, because her father had never been there. "You can't really join the club," she teased, "unless you go through the initiation ceremony."

"What do I need to do?"

"Are you sure you want to join? This club has nothing to do with insights into the life and times of the famed Woodrow Locke. Still interested?"

"Yes." His answer was so quick that she didn't doubt its sincerity.

Placing the candle between them, Mollie recalled their initiation rites. "You must answer my questions. First, tell me who you are."

"My name is—"

"No," she corrected. "You aren't facts and dates. You have to tell something secret about yourself. Something that nobody else knows about you."

Flynn concentrated. His mind filled with images from his travels. The Eiffel Tower at dawn. The verdant green of the Irish countryside. What were his secrets? He thought of the sea, the coral depths he'd explored in scuba gear and the roiling waves in a storm. Slowly he began to speak. "I'm afraid of the dark. Not the dark that comes with night, but fog that keeps me from seeing clearly."

"Continue."

"During my maiden voyage in the sailing craft I'd built myself, I hit a thick fog near Seattle. Though I couldn't have been more than five miles offshore, I was so scared that I thought I'd die from fear. Instead of piloting my craft, I hid in the galley. Shivering."

"How did you come out of it?"

"I heard whale songs. Mind you, I don't really know if there were whales or not, but I distinctly heard a low, primal call that brought me up on deck. From there, I seemed to see a glimmer of light and made my way to safety."

Without casting judgment on his statement, she proceeded. "The next question . . . what do you bring to this secret place? That has to be something about your distant past."

A peaceful silence settled over them. Finally Flynn said, "I can't think of a thing. I grew up on a farm and it was dead boring."

Mollie laughed. "Does this mean I'm not the only one with a memory block?"

"I can remember, all right. But it's so dull."

"I repeat, what do you bring to this place?"

"A solid foundation," he said. "Endless days of repetitive chores. Rising at dawn to milk the cows and gather the eggs from the henhouse and sweep the porch. I also bring good health. On my parents' farm, I learned to care for my body and for the growing things around me. Including my brothers and sisters. There were five kids in our family, and I was the oldest."

"It sounds wonderful to me," Mollie said.

"Are you speaking from the initiation ceremony?"

"No, that's just my own observation. I would have loved growing up on a farm."

"That's ironic. I'd have traded with you in a minute. Back on the farm, all my dreams were about the kind of adventure and excitement that you probably took for granted."

"We don't have much in common, do we?"

"Not on the surface," he agreed.

Mollie cleared her throat. "On to the next part of the ceremony. You need to write your initials on the wall."

In a corner of the cave, she found a tree branch of appropriate thickness. "Burn the end of this stick in the candle flame and use the blackened point to write."

While he followed her instructions, laboriously burning and writing and burning again, Mollie thought about his answers to her initiation questions. Obviously he was a rebel. His lifelong search for adventure came as a reaction to his upbringing. As long as he was dashing around the globe, no one would ever accuse him of being staid or boring.

He completed the *F* and started on the *C*. Not the sort of man who would settle down, she thought. Commitment was not awfully compatible with adventure. He certainly wasn't the right man to fall in love with. Not unless she was prepared to have her heart broken.

"There," he said. "I'm finished."

"Welcome to the club." She solemnly shook his hand. When he tried to pull her closer, she broke away. "Now we're friends for life."

"Friends kiss."

"Yes," she said softly. "They do."

The candle flickered in the small moist cavern, lighting his rugged features with a mystical glow. Mollie rose up on her knees. She placed her hand on his shoulder and solemnly gazed into his eyes.

His hands touched her waist. There was no initiation rite for this. No ceremony. No promises.

Mollie welcomed his kiss. His lips moved against hers, firm and tantalizing with their pressure. When his tongue pried against her mouth, seeking entry, she gladly took him inside and responded with her own exploration. His mouth was hot and slick. She savored the texture as his warmth spread through her like a hissing fire within the damp cave.

Her arms slid around his neck, pulling him close until their bodies melded together. On their knees, their long bodies matching, she could feel his heat, his strength. Mollie was hungry for this euphoric sensation, aware of a fierce need to feel alive.

His hand gently touched her breast, and she groaned with pleasure and surprise. Flynn was a dangerous thrill, but for once in her life she was willing to take a chance, to abandon routine in favor of sensual pleasure. Only a kiss, she told herself, this was only a kiss.

Under his caressing fingers, her nipples tightened to small sensitive buds. Her entire body felt electrified.

When he lowered her to the floor of the cave, Mollie did not object. The cold rock surface contrasted erotically with Flynn's vibrantly alive body. He gazed down at her. Smiling, sharing a secret moment.

Her arms glided over his chest and over his shoulders. She pulled him close and he eased himself down, slanting his torso across hers. Again she kissed him, arching her body against his. Her long legs tangled with his, and she felt his erection. An answering tremble ached at the juncture of her thighs.

His hard strength and savoring mouth had caused a meltdown within her. She was fluid, floating weightlessly except for the unbearable tension of her taut nipples as they pressed against his chest.

Her back connected with a sharp edge of rock and she winced. Immediately he loosened his pressure. "Are you okay?"

Unable to speak, she nodded.

His blue eyes glistened, slightly unfocused. "I'd give a year off my life for a bed. Right now."

She smiled. Perhaps this wasn't the right time. And it certainly wasn't the right place. But she was glad they had kissed. She would treasure this magic forever.

"I don't want to stop, Mollie. I could kiss you forever."

She forced herself to sit up, held his face in her hands. "Not now, Flynn."

"But soon?" His eyes shimmered with a masculine heat that could only be described as sexy. "I'm an impatient man. I want to make love to you."

"And then what?" Wistfully she patted his cheek. Her body was racked with desire. But her logical mind had resumed control. "There's no future for us."

"I know that wasn't a friendly kiss. You want me, Mollie. As much as I want you."

"You don't know that," she refuted. "Maybe you know all about my father, but you don't know me at all."

"I want to know you. Very much."

"More than finding *The Key*?"

Indecision flitted across his face, and she had her answer.

After blowing out the candle and replacing it behind the rock, she sidled past him, out of the cave and into the larger cathedral of rocks where the waterfall whispered moist, sensual suggestions that Mollie forced herself to ignore.

Flynn joined her on the ledge. "New York," he said.

It wasn't a question but a destination.

"Yes."

Colorado was bereft of more significant clues. Might as well try New York. Mollie already felt anxious. New York was one of the largest cities in the world, yet the isle of Manhattan was too small to escape her memories of Sergei and to find new pieces of her past. Manhattan was the place her parents' marriage had ended.

7

HOT, STEAMY SPRAY GUSHED from the shower head, splashing down Mollie's back and soothing her. A bathroom in a Manhattan hotel was not nearly as picturesque as her magical mountain cavern, but Mollie recognized definite similarities: the sensual trickle of water, a sense of privacy and her absolute confusion about her relationship with Flynn.

Yesterday, when they left the cave, she'd been an eyelash away from making love with him.

Last night, after he called his publishers to let them know he would be in New York, Flynn seemed distant and morose. Or had she been the moody one? In either case, Mollie spent the evening chatting with her aunt and uncle.

This morning on the plane, he had been preoccupied with sorting through her father's scribbled first drafts. And Mollie had slept.

Twenty minutes ago, he'd stormed out of her hotel room when she refused to attend the meeting with his publisher.

Ten minutes ago, he stormed back into her room to inform her that he understood her position. And he'd asked her to dinner.

During all that time together, they had not talked about her memories. Nor had they discussed their relationship.

What relationship? Mollie turned off the faucets and stepped out of the shower. Just because they'd shared the most incredible kiss she had ever experienced, it didn't mean they had a relationship. Or did it? Every once in a while, she'd caught him watching her warily, as if he were unsure. And that was an attitude she preferred to his regular bossy, arrogant self.

Flynn's behavior was enough to drive an organized person like herself to distraction. Which made her wonder why she was here in Manhattan, anyway. That silly little map her father had drawn told her nothing, apart from the fact that Manhattan was an island. And it had some connection with *The Key*.

Toweled dry and wrapped in a robe, she went to the window of her hotel room and opened the drapes to the dismal brick of the building next door. When she'd lived in New York City with her parents, their apartment had a panoramic view of Central Park. But the map couldn't refer to that apartment; it had long ago been rented to someone else. Then what did the map mean? There were no safety deposit boxes that Marscel didn't know about. No storage houses. No special family friends apart from the Marscels, and they certainly hadn't overlooked an unpublished manuscript.

Mollie sat on the edge of the bed. From memory, she punched out the Marscel's phone number. The housekeeper answered.

"This is Mollie Locke. Is Claudine home?"

"Mollie? They're supposed to be at a meeting with you. At some publishing house."

"Thank you."

Mollie hung up and glared at the telephone. The Marscels were undoubtedly at this meeting with Flynn and his publisher, and she didn't like the connotation.

Whenever John Marscel was involved, there was certain
to be a battle. She stared thoughtfully at her pleasant but
nondescript surroundings. This was a hotel room, not a
cocoon. Even if she barricaded the door and stayed inside, she wasn't necessarily safe.

The last time she'd been in Manhattan, Mollie had
been deceived by Sergei, her lover. She was older now
and wiser. That would not happen again. It was time for
Mollie to take action rather than sitting back and waiting for the world to disappoint her.

Quickly she dressed, applied makeup and left the
hotel.

Despite the blazing July heat, she strode briskly,
drawing comfort from the anonymous bustle of New
York City sidewalks. Among these throngs, there must
be others like her. By the law of averages, Manhattan
must contain another woman whose life paralleled her
own. The thought pleased her; Mollie had never wanted
to stand out in a crowd.

She found the publisher's building and marched inside. On the eighth floor, she spoke to a receptionist who
directed her to a conference room.

Though the door was closed, Mollie could hear
shouting from within. She recognized Flynn's voice and
Marscel's. With her hand on the doorknob, she paused.
A memory struck her. Mollie knew she'd been here before, listening to her father's rage in New York City. Rage
and sorrow. She fought the urge to run away. Instead, she
turned the doorknob; Mollie wasn't a frightened little girl
anymore.

The first thing she saw when she entered the conference room was a poster-sized book cover; *The Key* by
Woodrow Locke. She stared at the sketch. The fifteen
people in the room, including the Marscels, stared at her.

Claudine rose from her seat, came to Mollie and hugged her. She whispered, "You were wiser not to come. This is a melee."

Marscel boomed out, "Hey, Mollie girl. This is a pretty good turnout, eh? Old Woody can still pack them in."

"Yes," she tersely replied. She gestured to the cover sketch. "A foolish turnout if you're all here to discuss a book that probably doesn't exist."

"Exactly what I've been saying," Flynn muttered. He came toward her and pulled out a chair. "Won't you sit down, Mollie."

"I prefer to stand. I don't intend to be here long." Her gaze rested on a man who looked vaguely familiar. "Dr. Edleman."

"I'm flattered that you remember me."

The last time she'd seen him was the awards banquet, and he'd been flattened by Flynn. "I remember. Why are you here?"

"I'm an expert on your father's work. If *The Key* exists, I might be needed to verify."

"Hello, Ms Locke." A buxom woman introduced herself as a senior editor and said, "We're all so pleased to meet you."

Marscel chuckled. "As pleased as a pack of wolves meeting a lamb."

"Please explain," Mollie said. "Marscel?"

"In case it slipped your mind, this treasure hunt makes for some pretty exciting stuff. Even if you don't find *The Key*. I've already fielded two requests for your life story. And there's some fellow—" he pointed to a very young man who sat at the far end of the table "—who wants to make a movie about you."

"Me?" Mollie was flabbergasted. For years, there had been attention from researchers and the media. But it had always been about her father. She'd never considered herself newsworthy.

The editor explained, "Our hope is to publish *The Key*, but if your search fails, your own life story could make a fascinating book." She gestured to two neat men in matching business suits. "These gentlemen from marketing believe your biography could be a best-seller. And Flynn Carlson is the man to write it."

"I don't think so," Edleman said. "Flynn is too close."

"Please, Dr. Edleman," the editor reprimanded, "we haven't made any decisions yet."

"A biographer needs detachment," Edleman continued. "Flynn is obviously infatuated with this lady. He's not—"

"Excuse me," Mollie interrupted him. "Dr. Edleman, are you talking about writing my biography?"

"Indeed, I am. Quite a compliment to you."

"I haven't agreed to any such project."

She watched a sly grin spread across Edleman's face, and she recalled that he had written several unauthorized biographies, including the definitive work on her father. Consent of the subject was apparently of little concern to him.

Drawing herself up to her full height, Mollie vowed, "If you write one article about me, Dr. Edleman, if you write one paragraph, my attorney—John Marscel and his associates—will sue you for libel and harassment. I, personally, will make it my business to be the boot heel that grinds you into dust."

"Well, well." The editor cleared her throat. "Ms Locke, perhaps you would be more comfortable if Flynn—"

"I haven't contracted to write anything," Flynn snapped. "Only the authorized biography of Woodrow Locke."

"He wants more money," one of the marketing men said.

Flynn wheeled around and snarled, "Personal gain has nothing to do with it."

"Timely story," said the other marketing man. "But we've got to move fast. Alcoholism might not be hot by next year." He nodded to Mollie. "Your father was an alcoholic, wasn't he?"

The outright rudeness of his question threw Mollie off balance. Did everyone know about her father? She turned to Marscel and watched as he sadly nodded his head. That was absolute confirmation. Her father must have been an alcoholic if John Marscel, Woodrow Locke's greatest supporter, would not argue in his defense.

"Well?" the marketing man pushed. "That's a fact, isn't it? Ms Locke, do you yourself drink?"

Flynn answered, "That, sir, is none of your damn business. These plans are conjecture. And you can all go straight to—"

"May I remind you," the editor put in, "that you've accepted a sizable advance, Dr. Carlson. Plus monies to embark on this search for *The Key*. You are in violation of your contract by missing deadlines. We could demand repayment."

Marscel slipped into his attorney's hat. "Technically, Flynn, she's correct."

"We also publish your suspense books," the editor said. "I'm not threatening you, Flynn, but your cooperation here would be greatly appreciated."

Flynn rose to his feet. His gaze met Mollie's. Behind his anger, she saw a flicker of amusement.

"Ladies and gentlemen," he said, "allow me to show you what I think of your contracts. And of your fine, foundationless plans."

He rounded the conference table to the artist's sketch of *The Key* and took it off the stand. He held the sketch for a moment, then grinned at Mollie. "A very wise woman once told me that a missing manuscript from Woodrow Locke was not important. People's lives are important. Honesty and integrity are important. Another novel from Woodrow Locke is merely... interesting."

He ripped the poster in half.

Claudine Marscel applauded.

Before the two halves of *The Key* had fluttered to the floor, Flynn took Mollie's hand in his. "Shall we go?"

"Immediately."

Shouted threats accompanied their progress down the hall, but when they stepped into the elevator and the doors wheezed shut, Flynn burst into laughter.

"I don't believe you," Mollie said. "Didn't you hear all that stuff? You're looking at lawsuits. You're laughing as your writing career goes up in flames. Are you crazy?"

"Not anymore."

Flynn led her through the lobby and onto the street. It was muggy and hot. Daylight had faded to an ugly gray. The sidewalks were packed with marching hordes of commuters heading for home. But the world looked beautiful to him. The pressure was gone. He was free. "I know it's a bit early," he said. "And, as you just heard, my financial resources have just been severely depleted, but I would like to take you to dinner."

"I'm not exactly sure that I want to share dinner with you," she said. "It seems to me, Flynn, that you've been deceiving me, making promises without consulting me. Like the Mollie Locke life story?"

"I'd never write anything about you without your consent."

Her pace along the sidewalk was swift, and her heart hammered in double time when she thought of the intimate secrets she'd revealed to Flynn. Her uncle's alcoholism. Her cave. Her kiss. She must have been blind to trust him.

At a street corner, he turned to her. "I won't betray you, Mollie. You just heard me kiss off some very big bucks in that conference room. Because you were right. There are things more important than publishing."

She stormed across the street. "Such as?"

"My own integrity. I'm done playing games so that the publisher will finance me. And I won't push you to remember things until you're ready." In a matter-of-fact voice, he concluded, "I don't want to hurt you. Not for all the literary fame and fortune in the world."

"What about *The Key*?"

"What about dinner?" he said.

"I'm too furious to be hungry."

Mollie's strides couldn't keep pace with the charging emotions inside. She'd known from the start that Flynn was using her to find information about her father. She'd agreed to that, hoping she'd find solace in reviewing her past. But the thought of her life story being portrayed in a book—or, heaven forbid, on the screen—was not part of the bargain.

She blurted, "Why did you kiss me?"

"Mollie, could we please stop running down the sidewalk?"

"No. Did you romance me so you could add a section of lust to your book?"

"I'm not writing a book about you."

"Why not?" Her anger flip-flopped contrarily. "Am I not interesting enough? Not deep enough? Not sexy enough?"

"Lady, you are the sexiest woman I've ever known." He grasped her hand and pulled her into a small alcove beside a store window. "If we had met in another way, I would have romanced you weeks ago. It has taken every ounce of my willpower not to seduce you." He tilted her chin up and gazed into her face. "I care about you, Mollie."

"How can I believe you?"

As he watched, her lovely green eyes filled with moisture, and Flynn felt her pain. He'd been a great stupid fool not to explain his problem with the publishers, not to confide in her. "Believe me because it's true."

She raised a finger and wiped away her tears before her mascara was destroyed. "I'll tell you what's true, Flynn. The only reason you're with me is because I'm Woodrow Locke's daughter."

"Not anymore. Searching for *The Key* brought us together, but it's not why I kissed you. And it's definitely not why I want to be with you now. Give me a chance."

Part of her mind wanted to trust him, but Mollie held back. She swallowed the lump in her throat. "That's a beautiful line of blarney, Flynn. You must be part Irish."

"Irish and Swedish. And I'm not lying."

"If that's so, let's stop looking for the manuscript, shall we? Let's forget it was ever written. You stop being Woodrow Locke's biographer. I'll stop being his child. Let's call off this ridiculous search."

"I won't do that."

"I see." With slow resignation, she concluded that there was nothing between them except for her past. "Thank you for being honest."

"We have to find *The Key*," he said. "And my reasons aren't what you might expect."

"I don't want to think about it right now."

"But you can't help it, can you? Your past is always there." He touched the furrows in her forehead. "Your past stands between us as sure as the Hudson River separates Manhattan from the mainland. We can bridge the river or tunnel beneath it. But we will never truly connect until we've dealt with your past."

"Sounds hopeless. Dragging an island back to the mainland."

"I'd move Manhattan for you."

Despite her confusion and pain, Mollie chuckled. "That's a mighty fine boast."

"Finding *The Key* is an answer for both of us. It will satisfy my curiosity. And it might save your life." He took both her hands in his. "There's no chance for us unless we search."

Behind him, the crowds of Manhattan filled the streets, but Mollie saw only the promise in his eyes. In a subterranean corridor of her mind, Mollie knew he was correct. She couldn't abandon the quest until she'd reached a sense of completion. "All right, Flynn. I'll do it."

But when he leaned toward her for a kiss, Mollie raised her hand, touching her fingertips to his lips. "Not here," she said. "Not now."

He nipped at her fingers. "Later, Mollie. But first, I promised dinner."

Manhattan offered the most succulent and varied menus in the world, but Mollie felt incapable of making a decision. She allowed herself to be led to an unremarkable café near Rockefeller Center and ordered salad, wine and cheesecake.

When the waiter departed, Flynn raised his eyebrows. "Salad and cheesecake? Is that the sort of thing you'd order as a child?"

"Yes, except for the wine." She frowned. "Are we starting on memories again, already?"

"We have to be expedient. That map indicated that Manhattan has some significance for *The Key*, and I don't have the finances to stay in New York for long."

"May I eat in peace?"

"Of course." He checked his wristwatch. "Half an hour?"

"I thought you weren't going to push," she reminded him. "Patience, patience."

"You're right. And I'm sorry." He leaned back in his chair and fidgeted. "Whenever you're ready."

When their wine was served, Mollie closed her fingers around the glass. The blushing liquid sparkled in her hand. Sweet harvest of the grape. Nectar of the gods. What made the difference between a connoisseur and a drunk? She lifted the glass to her lips and took a delicate swallow. "Do you think there's a genetic basis for alcoholism?"

"I'm afraid so."

She took another taste of wine, trying to savor the aroma while suspecting that she was inhaling poison. "Thank goodness, I didn't inherit my father's drinking problem."

"What did you inherit?"

"How am I like my father?" Dismissively she said, "I'm tall."

Mollie took another sip of wine, then dug into her salad.

"What else?" he prodded.

"You're pushing again."

"Sorry."

Flynn controlled himself until Mollie finished every delectable bite of her cheesecake. The moment her fork hit the plate, he said, "The major event that occurred when you lived in New York with your parents was the divorce. I know the grounds were irreconcilable differences, but tell me about it from your perspective."

She sighed. "I remember the year in New York as being a special time of companionship for me and my mother. We were together a lot. I suppose she was so fed up with being treated like my father's appendage that even the company of a seven-year-old was preferable."

Flynn ordered two cappuccinos from their waiter. "You haven't said much about your mother."

"She didn't seem relevant to finding *The Key*. And I'm not so confused about Mother. She was a socialite. And beautiful. I have the feeling that if she'd lived, we would have been great friends when I was thirty. But she didn't have much use for a child. Still, I never doubted that she loved me. Even after she remarried, I had every advantage that money could buy."

"Did your advantages make you feel guilty?"

"Yes. I mean, what right do I have to feel sorry for myself? My food and shelter were lavishly taken care of. I saw the world, received an excellent education at boarding schools. I was never beaten, never molested."

"There are all kinds of abuse. Not all of them are physical. In some ways, your father was a genius. Certainly, he was clever enough to delude himself into thinking that his alcoholism was not emotionally abusive. Not to himself. Or to you."

Their cappuccino arrived, and she tasted it. "I did okay."

"You sure as hell did. You're tough."

She glanced up sharply, then grinned at Flynn's frothy white cappuccino moustache. She reached across the table and dabbed his upper lip with her napkin. "It's strange to be telling you these things. Feels like I'm betraying the family secrets."

He caught her hand. "Try to forget what happened in the publisher's offices. Mollie, I swear on my lust for you that I will not print your memories in the biography without your permission."

Her senses went zinging up and down like a yo-yo as she reclaimed her hand and held it on her lap. She couldn't understand how such a simple gesture had started such a potent reaction. It must have been his magnetism and the warm glow from his eyes. Slowly she said, "If you promise to consult me after writing the biography, it means that you plan to see me after our treasure hunt is over."

"That's right."

It was just possible, she thought. A relationship with Flynn might just be possible. Mollie concentrated. She really wanted to find the manuscript, to see the ecstatic expression on Flynn's face when she placed it in his hand.

"All right," she said. "Let's be methodical about this. I will list the places I remember from my childhood, and we can visit them tomorrow."

He sat at attention, listening. But Mollie was silent.

She remembered their apartment, but that was a dead end. And the Marscels' home. Finally she said, "Greenwich Village. I know my father had lots of friends who lived there. Maybe we should go tonight."

They left the restaurant and Flynn hailed a taxi. He instructed the driver to take them to the great arch in Washington Square. Though more touristy than Mollie recalled, the curio shops were still eclectic and interesting. The denizens ranged in style from punkish to high fashion. And the winding streets held an Old World flavor.

"These friends?" Flynn queried. "Do you remember anyone special? Any names?"

She shook her head. "Marscel would know better than I."

The streets held no memories. Mollie paused outside a bookstore window and stared at a prominently displayed copy of her father's posthumous book, *Gateway*.

"Love poems for an ex-wife," she said sardonically. "What a pitiful excuse for a book. My father really was a hopeless romantic when it came to women."

"And for his family. He wrote a whole novel for you."

"Maybe."

The nameless tune resurfaced in her mind. This time, however, she knew some of the words. Quietly she sang, "Longitude and latitude are more than just a platitude."

"What, Mollie?"

"It was a nonsense song my father wrote for me. I remember sitting at the piano and singing about north and south."

Flynn stood still and quiet beside her. "What else?"

"Up and down and round," her voice faded away. "I can't think of it. Maybe if I could play the tune . . ."

"Hold that memory." He pulled her into the bookstore and charged up to a clerk. "We need a piano. Right away."

"I've got sheet music."

"You don't understand." Loudly Flynn announced to the people in the shop, "I need a piano. Right now. I'll pay one hundred dollars."

"You got it, pal," said a dark-eyed young man wearing a black muscle shirt. "My place is two blocks away."

"Let's go," Flynn said urgently.

"Let me see your money first."

Flynn opened his wallet while he rushed the man out the door. They followed him to a steep-roofed brick house a few blocks away, then up the stairs to an incredibly untidy apartment on the upper floor.

A tired-looking redheaded woman came from the bedroom as they entered. "Jerry, who are these people?"

"This guy wants to use my piano."

The redhead shrugged and flopped onto the sofa.

Flynn sat Mollie down at the piano bench. In contrast to the rest of the cluttered apartment, the piano was well dusted. Flynn noticed a handsome guitar in the corner. "Are you a musician, Jerry?"

"Student. At Julliard."

Mollie plinked out the silly tune and hummed, but the words wouldn't come. "I can't remember."

"Try it again."

"Longitude and latitude are more than just a platitude." Her fingers kept playing, but the words escaped her. "Something about degrees and up and down. And every time I say 'up,' I hit this real high note, the highest note on the keyboard."

"Strange song," Jerry said.

"The man who wrote it was an author," Mollie informed him. "Not a musician."

Flynn placed his fingertips on her shoulders, willing his energy into her. "Calm down, Mollie. And think. Can you visualize where you were when you learned this song? Were you here in New York?"

With startling clarity, she remembered the main room of their 1968 New York apartment, done in pastels the color of dawn. There were flowers in porcelain vases. And books. And a rosewood spinet piano. Her mother shouted from another room about remembering to practice.

Mollie's fingers on the keys performed scales.

But the rosewood spinet wasn't the right piano. A hazy vision replaced the first. An old upright in a room that was all windows. Outside were tropical flowers and palm trees. Mollie could smell the ocean and hear the gentle lap of waves. "I was in the Keys. In Florida."

She heard her father's voice, telling her that she had to practice or she couldn't go out and play. In her mind, she reached up and started the metronome ticking like a clock.

She blinked. And the memory was gone. "I've forgotten."

"Try the song again."

She played it again. And again. It seemed to be no use, she couldn't think of any more words. Then her fingers froze above the keys. In sync with the odd tune, she sang the last verse. "Though we may someday be apart, remember the chart and the rhythm of your heart."

A half memory compelled her to strike the high note on the piano six times at the finale.

"That's it," Flynn said. "The charted rhythm of your heart." He lifted her from the piano bench and swung her around in an embrace. "You've done it, Mollie. You've figured it out."

"Hey," Jerry interrupted. "You aren't planning to do anything else in here, are you? Because I got to charge more if you are."

"Leave them alone," his girlfriend said. "They're cute. Tall, but cute."

Flynn looked into Mollie's eyes. "Want to try again?"

Exhausted, she shook her head. Though they'd only dashed two blocks through Greenwich Village, she felt as if she'd been on a treadmill for years. "I'm tired."

Flynn held her protectively. "I'll take you home."

After paying off Jerry and walking a short distance, he caught a cab and they returned to the hotel. As soon as he opened the door to Mollie's room, she stumbled across the floor and collapsed across the bed.

He sat beside her, lightly massaging her back and planning. "Tomorrow, we'll go to the house in the Keys. This seems almost too easy, doesn't it?"

"No. We still don't know where to look."

"You'll remember, Mollie. The secret has to be in that song. Some kind of chart. Maybe a boating chart. With longitude and latitude."

With an effort, she rolled onto her back and looked up at him. She was pleased because Flynn was pleased. But a cold echo of fear sounded within her. Mollie wanted nothing more than to sleep. For about two hundred years.

She closed her eyes.

The first sound she heard the next morning when a dull gray light oozed through her hotel room window was Flynn's baritone voice humming the nonsense tune.

Mollie yanked a pillow over her head. Though she couldn't explain why, she was angry.

8

MOLLIE DIDN'T WANT to get out of the bed. Not even the aroma of coffee inspired her. The way she figured, her mind had traveled through twenty years, all the way back to her childhood when she'd played the piano for her father. Wasn't she entitled to a brief hibernation? If not, it was only right that she be grouchy as a grizzly bear.

Flynn's cheerfulness didn't improve her mood.

"It's seven o'clock, Mollie. Time to get up and at 'em."

"How did you get in here?"

"I took your key last night after I tucked you into bed."

Mollie peered under the sheets. She was wearing her nightgown, but she didn't recall changing out of her street clothes. After she'd fallen across the bed, her mind was blank, and that was a scary prospect. "What happened last night?"

He placed a large cup of coffee on the bedside table. "Don't you remember?"

"How did I get into my nightgown?"

"Don't worry. Your virtue is intact. As exhausted as you were, you fought your way into the bathroom to change clothes where I couldn't watch."

"Good for me."

"Maybe not. I've heard that the chemicals and hormones released in the body during sex can prevent cancer."

Mollie stumbled from the bed. She was definitely not prepared for witty repartee at this hour of the morning.

A quick perusal in the bathroom mirror did nothing to lighten her mood. She looked like a zombie. Her mascara had smeared raccoonlike around her eyes. Her skin was about as fresh as the Dead sea scrolls. And her teeth felt furry.

She turned on the faucets for the bathtub. A hot bath could cure anything.

Immediately Flynn tapped at the bathroom door. "I'd appreciate it if you'd take a shower. Our plane reservations are for eleven o'clock, and I promised Marscel we'd visit before we left town."

She opened the bathroom door. "Plane reservations?"

"To Miami. Then we'll drive down to the Keys."

"Why the rush?"

He started singing, "Longitude and latitude . . ."

She eased the bathroom door closed and turned on the shower. That nonsense song was a clue, but there was still no guarantee that she'd remember the pertinent verses. Mollie stuck her hand into the shower and adjusted the water temperature while trying to hum the tune. There was nothing more irritating than a song lyric that was just beyond reach.

After the shower, the coffee and a neat application of makeup, Mollie felt more human. Not pleasant, but human. She breezed out of the bathroom, armed with logic. "Flynn, I see no reason for you to waste your money on a trip to Florida. Marscel and I combed the hacienda years ago and found nothing."

"True, but you really didn't know what you were looking for. If the so-called charted rhythms of your heart are longitude and latitude, it need only be a small notation. A sailor's chart. A few numbers and degrees."

"However," she continued coolly, "all that's really needed is for me to remember the words to that song. And I don't need to be in Florida for that."

When Flynn sat down on her unmade bed, Mollie had to turn away to keep from imagining what he would look like beneath the covers. He was dressed casually in loose-fitting beige slacks and a white cotton shirt that contrasted dramatically with his tan. Was he tan all over? Mollie pressed her fingertips to her temple, trying to reorganize her thinking. However, her sensual contemplation was a sign that she was feeling more awake. More aroused? A strange, impulsive urge struck her and she sat beside him. "Instead of the Keys, let's go to Maine where you live. I'd like to visit your home."

He looked pensive. "That's a tempting suggestion. But it doesn't have anything to do with finding *The Key*."

"Sure, it does. We can go there. I'll relax and I'm sure I'll start remembering."

When his arm draped casually around her shoulder, Mollie felt herself stiffen. She could feel that he was going to offer friendly advice. He was going to refuse.

"We need to settle this, Mollie. There are questions in your past that will haunt us until we find answers." He squeezed her close. "I want all of you. Not just the parts that your past will allow me to see."

"What if the hidden parts are ugly?"

"Then the other parts will be all the more beautiful in comparison." He traced her hairline with his fingertip. "Do you have any memories of Florida?"

"Of course I have memories about Florida. My parents and I lived down there in winters. And after the divorce, I spent summers at my father's hacienda. Alone with him. And the housekeeper, Marianna Escobar."

"What was it like?"

"Oh, I don't know. I used to climb trees and read books and swim and play with dolls. The usual things." She eyed him speculatively. "I'd rather go to Maine with you. Then I'd really have something to write in my diary."

"Your diary?"

She jumped off the bed and began to pace. "I can't believe I forgot it. Flynn, I kept a diary. I can remember writing pages and pages in the silly thing. A little red book. Or was it blue? I had it for years and years."

"Do you remember what happened to it?"

"I filled it up. I remember the last page." In her mind, she saw a white paper with fine blue lines and the careful cursive scrawl of a child. "I wrote; 'Not the end but a new beginning. Tomorrow I may find the mermaid's comb.'"

"Mermaid's comb?" Flynn questioned.

"It's a fairy tale. A mermaid can whip up a storm when she sings and combs her hair." Mollie knew herself well enough to interpret immediately. "The mermaid's comb symbolizes control—control of everything, even the elements. I don't know how many times I've wished for one."

"That's why you maintain this facade of superorganization, right?"

"It's not a facade."

Her life-style epitomized regularity and good planning. Her home was clean. The vast number of accomplishments at her job were testimony to Mollie's tidy efficiency. If only she didn't have anxiety attacks, her life would be perfect.

"No tension?" Flynn read her mind. "No stress?"

"Stress is an inescapable part of modern life." But Mollie knew she was covering up. Her outbursts and unexplained tensions were mere symptoms of the terror she felt inside. Sometimes it felt as though she lived in the eye of a cyclone, clutching frantically at pieces of order to keep the whole from spinning out of control and disintegrating into disordered nothingness.

"You weren't always so neat," Flynn informed her.

"And how do you know that?"

"I talked with Claudine yesterday, and she said you were a typically sloppy kid. Your mother complained about the way you wouldn't keep your room picked up."

"She did?"

"Don't all mothers? According to Claudine, your messiness was a major problem when your family was living in New York, because your apartment wasn't as big as a house. Apparently, you trailed your toys all over the place."

How delightfully normal, Mollie thought. Clashes with her mother about a messy room. Why couldn't she remember those things? Maybe Flynn was right when he said that she'd thrown out the good memories along with the rotten ones.

But there had been bad times. Especially in Manhattan right before her parents finally split up. There had been furious battles. Her mother throwing a vase. Her father kicking a chair. And there sat little Mollie with her toys, wishing she could control the world.

"I'm not messy now," she said.

"So? What about a trip to sunny Florida?"

"Why not?"

"It has occurred to me that there was a symmetry to our search. Your father might have liked the joke of hiding *The Key* in the Keys."

She stalked to the closet, flung open the door and got her suitcase. "I warned you before about trying to think like my father. It's impossible. He was not a rational man."

"Agreed. Hiding a valuable manuscript and planting the clue in the mind of a child is absurd."

"It's mean," she said, throwing the suitcase onto the bed. "It's like he's coming back from the grave and forcing me to remember him."

"The quest for immortality. Some men build monuments. Some write books." He caught a pair of sneakers that she flung toward the open suitcase. "Some men believe that by making love, they'll live forever."

"Fascinating." Her eyes narrowed. "And what about women? Don't women have a need to be immortal?"

"It's easy for a woman. She bears children."

"That's the most ridiculous notion I've ever heard. Mothers are immortal?" She scooped her clothes from the closet and threw them on top of the suitcase. "The male chauvinist in you is coming to the surface."

Flynn prudently stood up and headed toward the door. "When you've finished packing, meet me in the lobby and we'll go for a stroll through Central Park, then visit the Marscels."

"A walk? If we're in such a hurry, why walk?"

Flynn considered for a moment before speaking. He had wanted the visit to Central Park to be nonthreatening and unplanned. But it wasn't right not to explain. "When I spoke with Claudine, she recalled that your father often took you for outings in Central Park."

Her forehead wrinkled in concentration. Father-daughter quality time in Central Park? Though she had a misty recollection of wanting to play catch or take a walk, it didn't connect with her father. He'd always been too busy. Or too drunk.

An unreasonable anger churned her stomach—anger accompanied by fear. Intuitively she knew that something had happened to her in Central Park. Something awful. "Flynn? I don't want to go to the park."

"We're here in New York," he pointed out. "Might as well take the chance to do it."

"You promised that you wouldn't push me."

"I won't, because it wouldn't do any damn good. You've got to make the decisions on your own."

"I see. We're back to psychology, aren't we? The idea that the addict has to seek help for him or herself?"

"Are you familiar with Jungian psychology?"

"Vaguely. But you know my low opinion of shrinks."

"Jung had an interesting theory that people can only suppress their fears and desires for so long. If you don't deal with them, the unconscious rises up and drags you screaming and kicking to your destiny."

"Charming theory," she commented. "But maybe I'm not suppressing anything. It's just possible, you know, that I'm happy the way I am."

"Jung also said that there is no coming to consciousness without pain." He shrugged. "I won't force you to go to Central Park. And I won't drag you off to Florida. But you're going to have to deal with these fears sometime, Mollie."

He escaped from the bedroom and stood in the hall, listening at her door. Apart from the thumps and bumps of her vigorous packing, he heard no other sound. And what had he expected? Wild hysterical sobbing? A scream? Or had he expected her to burst into joyous song when he delivered his little Jungian lecture? He'd been fairly pretentious. A snotty professor in cap and gown, delivering his knowledge.

But what the hell? Flynn was a teacher. And a writer. And a man who cared about Mollie. That was the hardest part—his worry about the way she held herself so tightly in control. When her memories or real emotions bubbled out, she was horror-struck. Except for once. She hadn't been terrified by their kiss in that magical cavern in Colorado.

He smiled. That had been one helluva a fine kiss. Serenaded by the waterfall in the cool dark cave, her warmth had overwhelmed him. He'd never forget the feel of her body pressed close to his. Her soft flesh. Her long legs. And her passion. When her self-control lifted, she was an amazingly passionate lady. He sighed. The taste of Mollie had made him hungry for more.

Flynn straightened his shoulders and strode down the hotel corridor to the elevators. Though the barriers between them were high as the Rocky Mountains, though he was a naturally impatient man, Flynn knew she was a woman worth waiting for.

He brought his suitcase downstairs, checked out and sat in a comfortable chair facing the elevators. When Mollie appeared in her cool pastel skirt and overblouse, she seemed surrounded by softness. Flynn had to remind himself that the lady inside the delicate feminine packaging was tough.

She came directly to him. Her expression was tense, he thought. There was a tightness in the way she held her mouth. Her eyes seemed hard as emeralds.

"Okay, Flynn," she said. "Let's get this over with."

"We don't have to."

"Actually, I think we do." Her fingers knotted together. "There's something about Central Park that makes me crazy inside. And we never did find out why my father drew that map. There might be something significant to our search."

"Very logical," he said.

The flicker of a smile touched her lips. "Besides, I have no desire to be dragged, kicking and screaming, toward my destiny. I greatly prefer the dignity of choice."

While Flynn went to the hotel registration desk and arranged for her luggage to be collected and held behind the counter, Mollie perched on the edge of a chair. Unconsciously she pressed her fist against her waist and realized that her stomach was writhing with tension. She glared through the glass hotel doors to the drizzly gray weather outside. The ugly gloom suited her mood. Miserable. Hostile. Scared.

Flynn, on the other hand, was a regular Johnny Sunshine. There was a bounce in his step as he returned and offered his arm. "Shall we?"

"Maybe we need an umbrella."

"Let's pick one up at the gift shop."

"No, there's no point in getting an umbrella if we're leaving for Florida in just a few hours. But maybe..."

"Mollie, you're dithering. Do you want an umbrella or not?"

"I'm sorry. I'm just a little irritable, okay? Maybe you ought to keep your distance, Flynn."

"Never. I don't want to be distant from you."

Mollie led the way out of the hotel. Though Flynn had been pleasant this morning and hadn't really done anything to offend her, she was on the verge of exploding at him. A bad sign, Mollie thought. The park must hold a terrible memory. Her self-control had slipped so much that she couldn't even manage ordinary civility.

On the street, he took her arm. "I won't tease. And I won't lecture. I'll be quiet, and I'll be here for you."

They walked the few blocks to Central Park in silence, keeping step with other pedestrians who stirred the sticky Manhattan humidity that heralded a summer storm. Mollie could almost feel the pores of her face clogging as she strode along the busy sidewalks.

On the south end, they entered the park and wandered aimlessly past meadows and fountains. From the zoo, Mollie heard the roar of a jungle cat transplanted in New York City. Above them, all around, she saw skyscrapers silhouetted against the darkening clouds.

Slowly she recalled, "We came here. My father and I used to come here on the weekends when there were lots of people. We'd play catch with a baseball. I liked it, but I wasn't very good." She gave a small shrug. "I throw like a girl."

"You are a girl."

"Woman," she corrected.

"Not back then," he said. "You were a little girl. Do you remember?"

The mists shrouding her memories parted, and Mollie saw clearly. As a skinny kid, she'd walked through Central Park, holding hands with her father. He was telling her something important, but she wasn't really paying attention. "He always talked a lot," she said. "And we saw horses—policemen on horses. Not far from here, tnere's a pond with ducks."

"Did you come to that spot often."

"Only once." A harsh realization struck, and she froze on the walkway. "At the duck pond, he told me. That's where he told me that he was leaving. My mother was divorcing him."

"I'm sorry, Mollie."

She heard Flynn's voice as an echo. The other people in the park faded to shadows beneath the low clouds. Her reality was occupied with a time long ago. "It shouldn't have hurt so much," she said. "I'd been separated from him before when I was at boarding schools. But this was different. He was never going to live with Mother and me ever again."

She could see him, standing there, orating. She gasped, held her hand over her mouth to keep from screaming.

"What is it?"

She lowered her hand. "When he told me, he was drunk."

A core of bitterness erupted within her and she stalked off the path, across the grass, aiming unerringly for a small duck pond. Flynn stayed right beside her.

At the pond, she grabbed a stick, and with great force, flung it into the water. Her mouth tasted sour. "He was so drunk he couldn't stand up. He lay right over there on the grass and told me that he had to leave. Of course, I could come and see him. I could visit. And wouldn't that be fun. We'd go to the hacienda in the Keys and spend the day fishing. Fun! Playing in the damn sunshine, eating oranges and kiwi."

She went to the spot where her father had sprawled on the grass, lazily propped up on one elbow. Twenty years ago, yet she remembered with such perfect clarity that it was almost as if she'd been preserving this ugly memory under glass, like a precious artifact in a dusty museum. She'd been waiting for the right person to share it with. Flynn? Why should she trust Flynn? He had deceived her. He was using her.

Yet she was so relieved when he stood beside her and said, "Tell me, Mollie."

"The first time my father told me, I didn't believe him. Then he said it again and again until it sank in." She wheeled around and faced Flynn. "It was my tragedy. Mine. I was only seven years old. But I had to take care of him. He was crying." Her voice grew louder. "Put that in your biography, Flynn. The legendary, macho Woodrow Locke wept like a baby. And I had to help him get home. I put him to bed. I kissed him goodbye. And the next day, he was gone."

Remembered fury tore her guts. She wanted to shriek, to cry, to break something. But she was as helpless now as when she was a child. More helpless now because her father was dead. She couldn't blame him or curse him. He was gone.

Flynn reached for her, but she recoiled. "Don't touch me."

"It's all right."

"I need to finish this. I need to remember. There was something about a book. Maybe *The Key.*" She looked up at the gray sky. "I can't remember exactly. But he said something about how he would always love me, but he'd have to explain in a book that was especially for me. And I told him I didn't want his damn book. I wanted a father. If he gave me a book, I'd burn every copy. I'd throw it in the duck pond. He said that someday, when I was grown-up, I'd understand."

She turned away from the duck pond and went back to the meandering walkway. Now she was ready to return to the present, to get on with her life. "That's everything I remember."

"Take your time. This doesn't have to be done efficiently."

"Why shouldn't it be?" Yet she felt tentacles of emotion clinging to her, pulling her back. "My father must have been talking about *The Key*, and he drew a map of Manhattan so he'd remember his promise. Possibly, he hid the dumb manuscript because he was so paranoid that he actually believed that I would destroy it."

"Would you have destroyed it?"

"Yes." Mollie pressed her lips together. Too many words. She'd said enough. She should close the door before she said something she regretted.

Yet her words continued, "He'd call me his 'Green Eyes' and his 'babe,' his 'love.' And all the time, he was planning to leave. To run away like a coward." A wave of remembered emotion washed over her, and Mollie talked fast, trying to keep her head above water before the undertow sucked her down to cold oblivion.

"He cheated and he lied. He'd promise to take me swimming or promise to play catch. But promises never happened. Tomorrow never came. It was impossible to plan, because he always forgot. Except for his writing. He always found time for his writing. And for the booze in his bottom desk drawer."

Flynn placed his arm around her, snuggling her close to his chest. "It must be hard for you when other people—asses like me—tell you what a noble genius he was."

"He was a drunk. A disgusting, weak drunk who didn't have the courage to love me."

She closed her eyes and leaned against Flynn. Long-forgotten images raced across her mind. Her father's boisterous laugh. His ravings. She saw him in a hundred different poses. Sleeping. Dancing. Drinking. Playing catch. Fishing from his boat. Writing.

She pressed her hands tightly together, trying to catch her emotions and bring them under control. But it was too late. Impotent anger surged through her. "How could he have done that to me? He must have hated me."

"He hurt you, Mollie."

"What did I do wrong?"

"You're all right. You didn't do anything bad."

"But I hated him." No, that wasn't right. She couldn't have hated her own father. "I truly hated him. I despised him so much that I wanted to kill him. And then, he died."

"It's okay, Mollie."

She shuddered convulsively. "I didn't mean to say that."

"Of course not."

The dark clouds above Manhattan shot thunderbolts across the skies, but the rain fell gently. Mollie allowed Flynn to help her find shelter on a bench under a spreading oak tree, and they huddled together, watching the storm as it washed the dirt from the air, leaving the city clean.

Mollie rested her cheek against Flynn's chest. Though he was a comforting presence against the storm, he could not cure her poisonous memories. She felt her anger fading. Inside her was a hollow stillness. Her heart was empty.

Her sigh came from deep within. "I don't want to visit the Marscels, okay?"

"Sure." He shifted position to ease her more comfortably against his body. "What about Florida?"

"I don't want to go there, either. Which probably means that we should."

Flynn tightened his arms around her. More than anything, he regretted his glib statement about consciousness coming only through suffering. He didn't want to see Mollie being hurt so terribly.

"I didn't want to come to Central Park," she said. "I didn't know what was here, but I felt a terrible foreboding. And I have the same sense about Florida."

But did she want to continue? She closed her eyes and searched her soul. To this point, the journey had been painful, but she knew that it wasn't complete. "I need to go on," she said. "There's something else I need to find."

Fear mingled with anticipation as she thought of her father's hacienda in the Keys.

9

THE HACIENDA. Mollie had a fairly clear vision of her father's home on Stamper Key for it had formed the backdrop for many family photos. More than the house itself, she recalled the long tedious journey into the Florida Keys.

After the flight to Miami and hiring a rental car, she fastened her seat belt, glanced at Flynn and asked an eternal childhood question, "How much farther?"

"I was hoping you could tell me."

"It used to take forever," she said. "As a little girl, I remember sitting in the back seat of the car, staring at what was probably a magnificent landscape and being bored to death."

"I've only been to the Keys once before," Flynn said, "but I think we go south to Highway One."

"Whatever."

Her nonchalance worried him. After the outburst of intensity she'd displayed in Central Park, Mollie had seemed listless. On the plane, she'd picked at her food, read the magazines and generally dodged every pertinent question he asked. Though her manner was quiet and agreeable, quite without the usual sarcasm, she wasn't like herself, and he missed her feisty attitude.

Before he started the car, he studied her blank expression. Her luminous green eyes were dull and murky. "Are you okay? You're beginning to make me nervous."

"I'm fine," she quickly assured him.

"But you're so subdued. You haven't snapped at me in hours."

Her smile was as unreal as the painted smirk of a mannequin. "I guess I'm not quite all here. It's like waiting for something to happen. I've started on this complicated journey, and I'm not sure what lies ahead."

"Do you want to turn back?"

"Not now. It took me twenty years to get to this point."

Flynn started up the car and proceeded through Miami. He didn't know what to expect from this new incarnation of Mollie, and the unpredictability bothered him. Was her mind really blank? Waiting? He didn't believe it possible to go from the apex of emotion to lethargy in the course of one day. And so he called on her more familiar identity. "Mollie, I need you to do your organizational thing."

"Certainly." Her posture straightened. She ran her hand across her hair, smoothing the brown curls into shape. Her eyes were immediately sharp as she became all efficiency. "What shall I organize?"

Her transformation was so sudden that Flynn had to laugh. "Unbelievable."

"What are you talking about?"

"In the blink of an eyelash, you changed from being pensive and weird to this paragon of absolute order. It's like when Clark Kent used to run into a phone booth, then burst out as Superman."

"I was not pensive and weird," she said. "And, in case it has slipped your notice, I'm not physically equipped to be Superman. Or Clark Kent for that matter."

"Fine. You're Super Mollie. Just please stay in that identity. We need to make plans."

"You're right. I should telephone Marianna in Key West to find out how to get inside the hacienda. Then, we need Florida clothes. And, I'll arrange for somewhere to stay. It's not snowbird season, but the Keys are always pretty well booked."

South of Miami in Biscayne Bay, they stopped in a coffee shop and Mollie assumed possession of the public telephone while Flynn ordered two coffees and Key lime pie.

Though the shop wasn't on the beach, there was a seagoing atmosphere to the place. Fishermen's nets draped one weathered plank wall. And a display of watercolor artwork featured sailing ships and blue tropical vistas. Beyond the many windows, Flynn saw ferns and hibiscus and, of course, the ubiquitous Florida palm trees.

Woodrow Locke had chosen well, Flynn thought. To live beyond the tip of Florida, surrounded by ocean and sunrise, could be a lushly satisfactory life-style. He was eagerly anticipating his first view of the ocean and a chance to explore the islands with Mollie. And finding *The Key*, he reminded himself. That was, after all, the main reason they were here.

She returned to the booth by the window. "I finally got ahold of Marianna," she said. "I've had her address forever, because I always send her a Christmas card with a picture of snow on it, so it was easy to get her telephone number—even though there were ten other Escobars in Key West."

"Good work." He signaled to the waitress to refill his coffee mug. "And what did Marianna say?"

"Guess where we're staying tonight."

"From the smug look on your face, I assume you've pulled off a coup. Somewhere on the beach? Dangling from hammocks in a mangrove tree?"

"Yuck, no. Mangroves are swampy." Mollie announced, "We are staying on a fishing boat."

"But fishing boats usually come equipped with fishermen." He'd been looking forward to spending more time alone with Mollie. "Will they be willing to take time off?"

"It's a little boat," she explained. "One of Marianna's cousins is gone for the summer, and his boat has been sitting empty except for occasional weekend excursions. She suggested that we come to Key West, pick up the boat and anchor off the pier at Stamper Key—it's within a stone's throw of my father's hacienda."

Relief spread through Flynn. Not only would he be alone with her, but they would be on a boat, gently rocking in smooth seas. Though he wasn't counting on romance, the idea of making love with Mollie while the setting sun painted the skies over the Keys was irresistible. Life wouldn't get much better than that.

She sipped her coffee, checked her watch and called for the check. "We'll pick up supplies here, then head down to Key West. I told Marianna that we'd be there before nightfall."

"Slow down, Mollie." He yawned. "Let's take out time, smell the frangipani."

But she had already snatched the check and was headed for the door. Flynn had no choice but to follow Mollie's whirlwind of action as she paid the cashier and zipped out the door. At the rental car, she paused, leaning against the door on the driver's side.

She held out her hand for the car keys. "Come on, Flynn, I'm anxious to get this part of my life over with."

Her green eyes snapped with vitality. She was ready to take on the world, and Flynn would not object. He'd gladly let her take the lead. At this point, the search for the manuscript was more hers than his own.

He placed the keys in her hand. "Don't speed."

Though she wasn't reckless, Mollie was fast. She drove to a small department store where they purchased cool, casual Florida clothes—including swimsuits, Hawaiian patterned shirts and baggy shorts. Then they hustled through a convenience store to stock up on fresh citrus fruit and soda pop.

After a quick glance at the map, she aimed the car along U.S. 1, toward the longest oceanfront highway in the world. From Florida City, the first stretch of the Overseas Highway plodded through a murky continuation of Everglades Swamp—thick grasses, jack pine and oaks and palmettos. Clumps of mangroves. The warm air and the smell of water oozed contentment for Flynn. This was desolate country, but exotic. And soon they would be driving across the sea on a ribbon of highway that divided the Gulf of Mexico from the Atlantic. Though he had never lived in southern Florida, he felt as if he were coming home.

"Wish I still had my boat," he mused.

"How could you afford a boat on a professor's salary?"

"I built it myself. A beautiful little sailboat. But you're right, I couldn't afford it. I ended up selling it to finance the rest of my life."

"Not to finance the search for *The Key*, I hope."

"No, I let the publishers foot that particular bill. Which is a decision I regret heartily."

Mollie recalled the unpleasant meeting in their offices and mentally seconded his disgust.

"Of course, I can always build another sailboat," he said, "But, oh, my, she was a beautiful thing. I called her

Dade Lady in honor of your father's short story about the rampage of a Seminole Indian woman in southern Florida."

"That was about revenge," Mollie said, thinking that vengeance was an odd christening for a sailing craft.

"I thought of it as bravery, a reclaiming of heritage. It's also one of the few stories your father wrote with a strong female protagonist."

"Is that what you're hoping to find with *The Key*? A strong woman character?"

"Maybe." His gaze spanned the horizon then rested upon her. "And maybe I've already found her."

"Not me." Mollie shook her head. "I'm not that strong. And I'm definitely not the Dade Lady."

"I hope not. She had to burn down half of Miami to get her point across."

Just outside Key Largo, they passed the southernmost Crocodile Crossing sign. Through Key Largo, past Pennekamp park, they swept out to the open sea. Since the Keys were protected from the Atlantic by a coral reef barrier, the waters were waveless as a clear aqua mirror that gradually became a sapphire horizon.

Only this morning, Flynn reflected, they had been in New York City. It was difficult to believe that these two worlds existed on the same planet.

He gave a groan of pure contentment, then leaned back in the passenger seat and stoked up a fat cigar.

Mollie wrinkled her nose. "When did you get that thing?"

"While you were buying out the swimsuit rack." He took a long puff, exhaled and clenched the cigar between his teeth. "Don't worry, Mollie. It's not a habit. I smoke cigars only for special occasions, like returning to the sea. This is magnificent, isn't it?"

"No comment." She sniffed disdainfully. "Do you have any other weird little habits or rituals that I should know about?"

With gusto, he quoted, "'I must down to the seas again, to the lonely sea and the sky, / And all I ask is a tall ship and a star to steer her by.'"

"Poetry?"

"Another ritual. I tend to wax poetic at seaside. And at sunsets. Hope you're not offended."

"I don't mind. As long as you don't quote Woodrow Locke." She stared straight ahead, following the highway. "Did you ever write poetry?"

"I have turned out my share of cornball, tortured poetry. Especially when I was in Paris. There's an aura about that city. The moment I saw the Eiffel Tower I had an unexplainable urge to rent a garret, guzzle anisette and suffer for my art."

"Did you?"

"I'm not made that way. Deep in my heart, I'm a commercial writer who is dedicated to being paid for my work. However, it was in Paris that I wrote my first suspense novel with guns and espionage and sexy women."

"I'm glad you're not artsy."

"I have my moments." He winked. "It was also in Paris that I posed in the nude for an art class."

When she laughed, with the breeze from the car window tossing her hair and the sunlight bringing out warm highlights on her cheeks, he was mesmerized. She was a handsome woman. So full of life. How could he have thought she was a tease? Or insincere in any way? Mollie was earthy and real as the tang of salt water in the air.

"It's good to hear you laughing," he said.

"It's good to laugh." She cast him a stern glance. "But let's have no more analysis, all right? Just smoke your silly stogie and enjoy."

Puffing on his cigar, he watched the blue skies and omnipresent waters as they passed from one exotic green island to the next. There might be emotional danger in the route they were planning to navigate. Like the jagged coral reefs that surrounded the Keys—those beautiful reefs had caused hundreds of shipwrecks. But Flynn didn't want to think about that now. For this moment, he was riding into an adventure with a beautiful woman at his side. Nothing deeper than that.

"We probably ought to stop by the hacienda at Stamper Key," she said. "To see if the pier has been washed away."

"The pier by your father's old house?"

She nodded. "I wonder what it looks like. I haven't been here in nearly thirteen years."

The highway meandered over tiny islands and always back to the sea. After the dramatic Seven Mile Bridge across Moser Channel, a note of excitement colored Mollie's voice. "There's Big Pine Key and Pigeon Key, a couple of others, then Stamper."

Flynn should have been thrilled to visit the home of his literary idol, Woodrow Locke. Instead, he was more concerned for Mollie. He didn't want her to be hurt anymore.

When she pulled off the highway and drove along a narrow two-lane road through the feathery coconut palms on Stamper Key, he said, "I don't think we should come here yet."

"Why postpone the inevitable?"

She guided the car down an overgrown driveway. Behind a chain barrier and a No Trespassing sign, she eased to a stop.

"Let's think about this," he said. "We really don't have to go in here just yet. You've been through a lot today and it might be more prudent—"

"Now you're the one who is dithering, Flynn. Why?"

He blew out a giant puff of smoke. "It's been nice to have you acting like yourself again."

"And you're afraid I'll turn weird and pensive?"

"Something like that," he admitted.

Her hands grasped the front of his wildly patterned Hawaiian shirt, and she pulled him toward her. Though he knew that he shouldn't romance her, Flynn couldn't resist. He willingly embraced her, mesmerized by the glow from her green eyes. When their lips touched, he felt a whiplash of excitement, stunning his brain with a sensual promise that was nearly as wonderful as the sea. She was fantastic.

Gently Mollie separated from him. "Thank you for thinking of me."

She climbed out of the car and slowly turned in a circle, surveying the forest palm, sapodilla and the banyan trees that spread a leafy umbrella above high hedges of red-orange hibiscus. A skinny little lizard raced across the long grasses and climbed a thick vine.

"You remembered the route easily enough," Flynn said. "Do you have clear memories of this place?"

"Don't forget that I came here with Marscel after my father died. I was sixteen, and I do remember that time."

She ducked under the thick steel cord that held the No Trespassing sign across the road. Stamper Key was familiar to her. More than anything, she recalled the scent of salt water mingled with a damp earthly aroma in the thick warm air.

She ran her finger across an unremarkable metal mailbox with "Locke" written on the side in block letters. "My mother hated it here because there was no social life. Key West is a good twenty miles farther on the highway, and the Conch fishermen weren't exactly her idea of culture."

She picked her way along the overgrown asphalt strip of driveway. "Marianna says the hacienda hasn't been kept up. She's had relatives living here from time to time, to keep an eye on the place and to clean up. But it's been mostly vacant."

They rounded a clump of palms and Mollie stood very still, gazing at grasses beneath her feet. She knew that when she lifted her eyes, she would see the hacienda. The home of her memories. The place where she had spent many long hours with her father. In her mind, the "longitude and latitude" nonsense song played counterpoint to the cries of terns and migrating tropical songbirds. Finally she was here.

Flynn took her hand. "Welcome home, Mollie."

Very slowly she tilted her chin up and opened her eyes.

10

THE TWO-STORY frame house had a wide veranda and balconies with wrought-iron railings. Mollie remembered the clean white paint with black trim, louvered shutters and dark gray shingles on the roof. She shuddered when she saw what had become of her father's hacienda.

Windows that had not been shuttered were boarded over. The paint peeled from the weathered, rotted wood. Rust corroded the gutters. The porch roof had half collapsed across the entryway. Latticework around the foundation's crawl space was torn. Ugly green weeds choked the land that had once been tended by a gardener, and the large oak tree in the front yard was defoliated, revealing the skeleton of a child's tree house.

"It used to be so pretty," she said wistfully. So long ago, when she was a little girl with her mother and father holding her hands, they had been a pretty family, standing on the porch of this house. "There were hanging flower baskets with azaleas and oleander."

But there must have been weeds. Even then, the weeds had been ready to strangle her memories, to hold fast while the damp fetid rot of the tropics spread. She gazed at the tumbledown roof.

"Hard to believe." She turned to Flynn. "It's still standing."

"It could be repaired," Flynn suggested, "if the basic structure is solid."

"Do you think so? It's a shame for a perfectly good house to go to waste." She turned away from the abandoned husk of her former home. "What am I thinking? There's no point in repairing it. I don't even know who owns it."

"You do."

"What?" She spun around and stared. "What do you mean?"

"You own this house and the land it stands upon. Marscel commented on the fact when we were going through your father's papers." He studied her closely. "Surely you knew about the hacienda."

"I didn't." Eagerly she went toward the house. It needed a complete renovation. But the hacienda was hers? "You must be mistaken."

"Marscel mentioned it more than once. Like you, he thought it was wasteful to leave the hacienda empty, but he said that whenever he spoke to you about it, your response was vague."

"I remember him asking what we should do about the house, but I never guessed that it was more than idle chat. Or that it was my decision."

Mollie surveyed the hacienda with a more speculative eye. Even if the house was beyond repair, the property on which it stood must be valuable. Surely she could do something useful with this land. Fix it up and sell it. Or donate the house to a worthy charity—arrange for it to be a foster home or a halfway house. Liana, she thought, would love it here.

Picking her way along the overgrown flagstone path, she circled to the rear patio. Was the structure sound? She needed to hire professional contractors to assess the damage. The slump of the roof, seen from the side of the house, was not encouraging. Many shingles were gone, probably blown away by high winds. But she spied a dormer with an arched window that was absolutely intact.

Flynn trailed behind her. "I can't believe you didn't know. You're so organized that I wouldn't expect you to lose a pencil. How could you misplace a house?"

"My father's estate was a mess. The only will he left had been scribbled out in a bar with a half-drunk attorney. And remember that there were three ex-wives, including my mother, who made all sorts of claims—not to mention the mob of drinking buddies and former lovers who he'd promised things to. At first, it didn't look like I'd inherit a dime. Then, for years afterward, I'd receive documents from Marscel telling me about new settlements."

"But a house? In the Keys?"

"Keep in mind that I was in my teens during a lot of this settling up. Plus, my mother's family was wealthy. I never needed money. After I put down roots in Chicago and had my life in order, I didn't care what my father had left. Half the time I filed the documents from Marscel without reading them."

Her forehead wrinkled in a frown. Her excuses still didn't explain such a huge lapse. "I doubt that Marscel ever sent the actual deed, because he's my attorney and keeps all my important legal papers."

"That doesn't sound like competent, capable Mollie."

"As you might have noticed." Sarcasm edged her voice. "I'm not terrifically efficient when it comes to dealing with my father."

But that wasn't the answer, either. Mollie knew it. She knew that she was making excuses to avoid the real reason she'd never taken possession of her old family home.

The rear of the house featured a huge concrete-slab patio bordered by Key lime trees, an overgrown courtyard and a stone sundial. Though this seaward side should have received the worst wear, it was protected by a wall of palms and banyans. The rear of the house was marginally less deteriorated than the entry. Mollie stretched out her hand and touched the weathered siding. Despite the radiance of Florida sunshine, the wood felt cold and dead.

"This is my fault," she murmured. "How could I have been so careless?"

For the first time, it occurred to her that her determined neglect of her past might have far-reaching effects—consequences beyond herself. If she had been more diligent in learning about her inheritance, she would have known about this house. During these years that it stood empty, the hacienda could have been used for something beneficial.

"Can't be helped." She turned on her heel and headed toward the lapping sound of the surf. "Let's make sure the pier is still standing and be on our way to find Marianna."

The weathered boat house and the pontoon pier appeared to be all right. The thick planks of the pier creaked and wobbled when she trod upon them, yet felt solid beneath her feet. She walked to the end and gazed at the vast blue sky and sea, meeting in a distant horizon. The Keys were such a strange place—swampy little islands strung together by the Overseas Highway—the home of turtles and porpoises and miniature deer and barracuda, but an unlikely habitat for man. Impractical, she thought, and precarious with coral reefs and storms to tear the hulls of ships.

But there was magic in the Keys. She didn't share Flynn's poetry-spouting enthusiasm, but Mollie found a soothing peace in this expanse of water and the distant strange mangrove islands.

Slowly she turned and looked back at the house. From here, with the upper eaves peeking above palm and banyan and shrub, the house wasn't so ugly. Some of the charm remained.

"It's not so bad," she said. "It can be fixed."

"It could be beautiful."

She looked up at Flynn. "If it weren't for you, I might not have come here until the house was rubble. Beyond repair."

Her mind cleared as she looked up at him, and she knew why she had not claimed this heritage before now. She had not been ready until Flynn came to guide her. His determination gave her a reason to search. His strength fired her own courage.

"Are you all right, Mollie?"

"It's not going to be easy," she said warily. "Putting it all back together."

"I'll help."

He stepped up behind her on the pier. His hands glided up and down her arms, caressing her from behind. She was glad that he'd chosen this moment to touch her. She needed his reassurance. As she stood on the pontoon pier, feeling the rhythm of the waters and gazing out to sea, being close to Flynn seemed somehow appropriate.

She hummed her half-remembered tune and recited the few verses before she shook her head. "I don't particularly remember anything. The shock of seeing the hacienda so tumbledown must have chased my memories back into their dark cave."

Her shrug eased her more snugly toward him. Her back found a comfortable niche against his chest.

His hands encircled her waist, and his fingers locked beneath her breasts, holding her. Mollie breathed deeply of the salty Key air. His body felt warm and substantial against hers. Solid. He gave her something to believe in.

She swiveled in his embrace and faced him. He looked very right in this sensual greenery. "You like it here, don't you?"

"I like being with you."

His mouth slanted across hers, arousing a quiver of anticipation that shot from her lips to her toes. Her body was assaulted with sensation, and the greenery seemed to surround her. Her mind was blank of any thought beyond the pleasure of his kiss. She savored his masculine scent mixed with the tang of sea air.

Her fingers caressed his thick blond hair and descended to his muscular shoulders. His body—long, wiry and slim—appealed greatly to her. Fate had been kind to make them partners.

Breathless, she drew away from him and called up her willpower. "We have to stop."

"Why?"

"Because if we continue, I just might want to make love to you. Then, I might want to make love again."

"That's fine with me."

"But we'll never get to Key West."

"There's always tomorrow."

"And we'll never find *The Key*."

She slipped out of his embrace and took two determined paces away from him. His magnetism enticed her, but she refused to be drawn. "I think I'm beginning to trust you. Isn't that amazing?"

"Why amazing?"

"Well, you're an admittedly irresponsible adventurer."

"I am?"

Her lips twisted in a wry smile. "Flynn, old pal, responsible people don't jump out of moving airplanes or take off sailing on homemade crafts or climb high mountains."

"Well, maybe they should."

"And I have other reasons not to trust you. You're a professor and writer who is preparing a biography of my father. And that is exactly the sort of person I've learned to mistrust." She cocked her head to one side and studied him. "Are you sure you don't have a stunt double who does that intellectual stuff?"

"Nope. Unlike you, Super Mollie, I'm Clark Kent in my daily life. And Clark Kent all the rest of the time, too." With a stride, he closed the distance between them. "I never claimed to be Superman. You might be wise not to expect too much from me."

"You're saying that it might be wiser not to trust you. Correct?" She stared directly into his eyes, wishing she could clearly perceive his motives. "Are you planning to betray me, Flynn?"

"Of course not."

She saw sincerity in his gaze, but his words were not reassuring.

"We both know that I might disappoint you. When this is over, after we've found whatever it is that we're going to find, we might go our separate ways."

"I understand. I am not projecting a future with you. No plans. *Nada.* Nothing."

"I don't want to hurt you."

He reached toward her, but Mollie quickly moved away. "Don't worry. Be happy. I'm living for today. Not tomorrow. Not next week. Not ten years from now." She checked her wristwatch. "And today we need to press on to Key West."

With a great show of energy, she marched up the path and around the house toward their car. He might leave; she might leave. So what! He was behaving as if she'd been trying to slip a ring on his finger. Or a noose around his neck. What was he afraid of?

"Ridiculous," she muttered as she climbed behind the steering wheel and headed back toward the highway. Somehow, the sun seemed less brilliant and the rippling of the waves described a grim monotony.

IN KEY WEST, Mollie received a terrific welcome from Marianna—a boisterous woman in a flower-splattered muumuu. With cries of delight, Marianna dragged them into her neat home and seated them at the well-polished dining room table.

"First, I will show you something." Her voice lilted between English, Spanish and Bahamian. "Then, my baby Mollie, we are going to eat."

Before Mollie could protest, Marianna thrust a dime-store photo album into her hands. Inside, Mollie's annual Christmas cards—each with a picture of snow—were displayed.

"My treasures." Marianna smiled hugely. "I've seen the frost and the snow on the ground when I visited New York City. In all my life, I have never seen the snow fall."

"Come visit me during January in Chicago," Mollie said. "I'll show you so much snowfall that you'll be sick of it."

"Don't be silly, child." She bustled toward the kitchen. "I can't leave my family for a whole month. Oh, they'd be crazy. Oh, my, they would starve to death."

Mollie knew better than to object. Marianna was a stubborn woman when it came to taking care of the people around her. Though she'd never had children of her own, she'd risen to the position of matriarch for the vast Escobar clan—a family of native fishermen and salvagers who proudly called themselves Conchs.

She returned with a bowl of fruit and sticky pineapple candy. "Eat. You'll come back here now, Mollie, to be fixing up your father's hacienda. And you must live there and take care of it. When empty? Oh, it is too impossible. Only last week, I went inside and tried to clean. Impossible."

"Inside?" Flynn questioned. "Is the house still furnished?"

"Oh, yes, in some rooms. I told Marscel about it. Years ago, he said I should take what I needed." She slapped the surface of the table. "I took this. I could not see this table get dirty and old with lizard footprints going up the middle."

"I'm glad you've taken things out of the house," Mollie said. "Otherwise, they'd be ruined. And I'm still not sure that any of this belongs to me."

The question of ownership had gone far enough. Mollie asked to use the telephone. After a collect call to Marscel that confirmed Flynn's statements, she walked through the kitchen to the dining table where Flynn and Marianna were cheerfully gossiping about Woodrow

Locke. Then she heard the familiar tune. Flynn was singing her "longitude and latitude" song to Marianna.

Mollie stood quietly and listened as Marianna denied any knowledge of it. "But Mollie and her daddy were always making up songs," Marianna said. "He loved to hear her play the piano."

Conflicting emotions welled up in Mollie. Though pleased with the idea of her father's approval, she was disbelieving. If he enjoyed her so much, why did he choose to spend his days with a bottle?

"Mollie?" Flynn called out. "Are you off the telephone?"

The sound of his voice startled her. She pasted on a calm expression and went to the dining table. "What were you two talking about?"

"Your treasure hunt," Marianna said. "I told Flynn that if he wanted a treasure to be found, he should announce it in Key West, an island full of scavengers."

"Exactly what Marscel was afraid of," Flynn said.

"What?"

When Marianna looked offended, Flynn explained, "Marscel was worried that the house would be looted and destroyed if anyone thought there was treasure there."

"Perhaps there are looters and smugglers on Key West," Marianna said archly. "But not in my family. The Escobars are fishermen and . . . entrepreneurs."

"I apologize." He looked expectantly at Mollie. "What did Marscel have to say?"

"You are supposed to get in touch with your editor immediately."

He shook off that bit of news with a casual nod. "What about the hacienda?"

"It's mine," Mollie replied. "The house, the furnishings and sundry other properties. Marscel couldn't believe that I didn't know. And, neither can I."

Perhaps it was just as well, Mollie thought. There had been times when she would have gladly taken a bulldozer to her father's home. And now? Now, she felt somewhat differently. Some of her anger at her father had been spent. Besides, it was silly to take out her feelings about him on a house. "Actually," she said, "I could learn to enjoy being the lady of this formerly splendid manor. And the other Florida properties that come with it."

Flynn questioned, "Other properties?"

"My father happened to be one of the great gullible purchasers of Florida swampland. I recall several trips to survey a new piece of land that turned out to be a half acre of useless marsh."

Flynn rose to his feet and swept a bow. "You might be a land baroness."

"Indeed, I might. I might be queen of the crocodiles and palmettos."

"Very exotic."

"But not very practical."

Marianna granted her benediction. "This is who you are, Mollie. Maybe you're all grown-up, but you are always your father's baby girl."

Certainly she couldn't deny the truth of Marianna's statement. She was Woodrow Locke's child, but she was also an adult, not a helpless innocent. Mollie was old enough and realistic enough to look at the hacienda as nothing more than a house. A valuable property that should be taken care of.

And if it were renovated? She could sell it. Or donate it to a worthy cause. An oddball notion whispered enticingly to her. What if she decided to stay here? It was just possible that she'd like living in the Keys, the land at the edge of the horizon.

11

THOUGH HER THOUGHTS REMAINED focused on a strange but somehow familiar horizon, Mollie managed the mundane business of going to the dock, unloading their supplies onto the old flat-bottomed fishing boat named *Sea Roamer* and handing over the keys for the rental car to Marianna. Before Flynn cast off, she suggested that they take a few moments and watch the sunset.

"I'd like to," he said.

"Can we go to Mallory Square?"

"Anywhere you want."

During their stroll to the square, they encountered a man selling "fresh catch" fish, another with a waist-length braid who offered "real" gold watches, and a crew of street musicians. In the square they joined a throng who waited in reverent silence for nature's show. Sunsets on Key West were an almost sacred ritual.

"Hold onto your wallet," Mollie warned.

Flynn nodded. He followed as she expertly threaded through the crowd to find a vantage point on a rickety wooden pier that seemed too fragile to support the weight of the many people who crowded onto it.

The irony of a Key West sunset was not wasted on Flynn. While the heavens were painted with pink and mauve and purest gold, the earth displayed a scene reminiscent of Hieronymus Bosch's painting of the *Garden of Earthly Delights*. Wide-eyed tourists gaped while the natives mingled among them, offering strange treats and illicit pleasures. The sultry air, scented with fish and sea and sweat, created a warm sensuality.

Key West was a place where normal conventions did not apply. A land of incredible beauty, of dreams that might suddenly become nightmares. A strange land, Flynn thought. And Mollie fit in perfectly. Though she thrived in Chicago's hustle, she was content to stand here on a pier, non-productively watching the skies. In the last glow of the sun's rays, her features relaxed. Her expressive green eyes were as serene as the sea.

The intensity of their search culminated within him, and he yearned for her. Tonight they would be alone on the fishing boat. Tonight he wanted to make love. More than finding *The Key*. More than anything. He wanted to caress her long legs, to taste her lips until he was satisfied. He wanted to become a part of her.

An impossible dream? Flynn knew he had to control his desire. Mollie was emotionally fragile right now.

When the sun finally descended below the horizon, like a drop of golden honey, the crowd applauded. Mollie sighed. "The next part of this ritual is visiting the bars on Duval Street. But I'd rather skip that."

"You like the Keys, don't you?"

"It's a great place to visit." They trailed among the sunset watchers. "But to live here? It's not exactly a center of commerce. How on earth would I make a living?"

"You could be like Marianna's family. An entrepreneur."

"A pirate, you mean." She chuckled. "That's not so different from Chicago. Except, in the city, the pirates wear business suits and carry attaché cases."

At the pier, Flynn sighted a swarthy man sitting on the deck of *Sea Roamer*. "Do you know him, Mollie?"

She shook her head. "But he's probably one of Marianna's relatives."

When they approached, the man called out, "Hey! Are you Flynn? The guy who's looking for treasure at the old Locke place?"

"There's no treasure," Flynn said as he crossed the gangplank. "We're looking for an old book."

"Oh, yeah? But maybe a book might be worth something." The pirate glanced appraisingly at Mollie. "You're Miss Locke, right? If you decide to fix the place up, you call on me. Rafael Escobar."

"I will," Mollie said. "But not if I find treasure hunters at the house. Because I'll know who sent them, Rafael."

"I won't tell anybody." He turned to Flynn. "There was a telephone call for you from some guy named Edleman. You want to know what he said? It'll cost ten bucks."

Flynn pulled out a ten-dollar bill and gave it to Rafael, who rattled off the message, "Marscel talked to an editor, and the editor talked to Edleman. And Edleman says that maybe you and him can work together."

"Swell," Flynn muttered. "I've always wanted to collaborate with a snake."

"You need a guide?" Rafael asked as he pocketed the ten.

"Not a chance."

"Okay." He hopped off the boat. "And I'm not going to tell anybody, Miss Locke. You'll remember me, huh?"

She nodded. As she watched Rafael hurrying down the pier, she said, "We'd better get moving, Flynn. The pirates are closing in."

"You're right. Frankly, I much prefer the native Escobar variety to Edleman."

While Mollie went below deck to find something for dinner, Flynn lit the running lights and maneuvered carefully through the crowded harbor into the open sea. He stood at the helm of the flat-bottomed fishing boat, struggling to gain perspective. Rafael was certain to alert every scavenger in Key West that there was something of value at the Locke place on Stamper Key. That was not so good. And why had Edleman called with an offer that Flynn was certain to refuse? That, Flynn decided, was extremely ominous. If *The Key* existed, they needed to find it right away.

But tonight? There was nothing to do but sail on. And make love beneath the blessing of a tropical moon.

As they skimmed the waveless waters, the stars overhead made Flynn's worries seem like petty folly. He enjoyed the way the thirty-five-foot fishing boat handled. Though it was over twenty years old and the paint was chipped and the deck railings were marked with rust, this craft had been well maintained in the ways that mattered. The engine purred. The navigating equipment was functional.

He powered the craft across the still ocean surface, keeping a careful watch for jags of coral reef. *I must go down to the seas again, for the call of the running tide, Is a wild call and a clear call that may not be denied.* Like passion. He could not deny his desire for Mollie much longer.

When she emerged from below deck, he surveyed her with great appreciation. The breeze from the gulf whipped through her hair. The pale moonlight illuminated her flesh. "Come stand beside me, Mollie."

She joined him at the helm, gazing straight ahead through the windshield. "These waters are amazing, aren't they. So smooth. Like a reflecting glass for the moon."

"You are amazing," he said.

"Oh, sure, I'm the eighth wonder of the world."

His arm circled her waist. "That's Stamper Key dead ahead."

They proceeded in silence. Mollie was very aware of his nearness. Tonight she would be alone with him.

Logically she should have been exhausted. This had been one of the longest days in her life. From Central Park, where she confronted her memories, to Florida, where she faced her father's hacienda. She should have been limp and tired. Instead, she felt alert. And filled with desire.

She cleared her throat. "I'd rather not go ashore tonight. That rotting house will be awful enough in daylight."

"Agreed." He squeezed her close to him and whispered into her ear. "For the next few hours, let's forget about *The Key* and all the pirates who are after it."

"Then what shall we think about?"

"Us."

Before she could respond or question, Flynn released his grasp and concentrated on bringing the craft around. She followed him out of the boat house. "May I help?"

He took her hand and led her to the deck railing. "I'd rather that you stand here like Queen of the Crocodiles, mistress of all you survey."

Mollie struck a suitable pose and waited while Flynn tended to the boat and dropped anchor a hundred yards offshore. The roof of the Locke hacienda was visible from their mooring place, but she turned her gaze away from the house. Not tonight. She would not be thinking about her memories tonight.

When he turned off the engine, she experienced a lovely stillness. Not a silence, for there was the liquid whisper of the waves and cries from island birds. Stillness, but not motionless, because of the gentle rocking of the boat. Yet, Mollie felt quiet inside. Her inner turmoil had lessened to a sigh.

Until Flynn approached her. In the moonlight, he seemed larger than life, magnetic. He was a conquering adventurer who would carry her to the most wonderful heights of passion. And yet she was more attracted to him because of his well-concealed sensitivity. Making love with Flynn would be different than with any other man. He had seen her at her worst. Her ugliest secrets were exposed to him, and he hadn't abandoned her. Though she could not expect a forever commitment, Mollie felt safe with him. In a way, their search had always been directed toward this moment.

In the shadow of Stamper Key, where she'd been a sad little girl, Mollie felt a woman's hunger as she peeped at him from beneath her eyelashes. His broad-shouldered stance bespoke the power of a man who nonchalantly undertook adventures like climbing mountains and swimming with sharks.

"Mollie?"

His voice was questioning, a bit nervous. She thought his tension was endearing. A warmth sped through her veins, but not the same kind of heat that had fueled her anger. This time, Mollie felt the rising of hot desire.

"Mollie? Would you care to go below?"

Below deck was a large hold for storing the day's catch, and a kitchen with propane stove, microwave and running water. There was also a cozy sleeping cabin that was swathed with mosquito netting. Mollie knew her choice of destination.

"I'd like that very much."

Her words seemed prim, but the emotion behind them was raw and wanton. As she descended the ladder to the ship's galley, she hoped Flynn wasn't thinking of dinner.

She paused beside the table and faced him. "Are you hungry?"

"Yes."

He surrounded her with his arms and kissed her with a passion that left no doubt as to his intentions. His tongue penetrated her mouth, teasing and exciting her. His large hand cupped her breast.

"Wait," she gasped.

"I want to make love to you, Mollie. Don't tell me to stop now."

"I haven't the slightest thought of stopping you," she protested. "But there is a perfectly lovely bedroom down the hall. Why don't—"

Before she could complete the sentence, he had moved down the small, narrow corridor and pulled her after him. In a single fluid motion, they entered the tiny cabin and tumbled across the bed. The moonlight through a porthole gave an ephemeral light to the room. Flynn rose above her, resting on one elbow.

When his lips neared hers, Mollie placed a finger across his mouth. "Tonight there will be no talk of missing manuscripts or memories."

"Not one syllable."

"And it's my turn first."

"Your turn?"

She sat up on the bed and pushed him flat. "Lie still, Flynn."

Carefully watching his pale blue eyes, Mollie unfastened the buttons on his shirt. In his gaze, she saw a touching uncertainty that inspired her. She'd waited so long to be with him that she wanted their lovemaking to take hours.

When she finished with the buttons and tugged the sleeves down his arms to bare his chest, Mollie lowered her mouth to his chest and nuzzled in the springy mat of dark masculine hair. Her lips found his nipple and she lightly sucked at the hard, dark button. Beneath her, she heard him catch his breath. His warm flesh seemed to tremble.

Slowly, sensually, she tasted his other nipple, circling it with her tongue. Her fingers raked lightly over his flesh and descended lower until she felt his hard, hot erection straining against the fabric of his shorts.

With a moan, she rolled onto her back, pulling him on top of her.

Flynn whispered, "Not yet, lady. Now it's my turn."

He quickly unfastened her blouse and cast the light cotton fabric aside. His thumbs lightly caressed the peaks of her breasts beneath her lacy bra, then he skillfully reached behind her back and unfastened the snap.

Her eyes widened. "You've done this before."

"I've always been good with contraptions."

With a flourish, he removed her bra. "Lie back, Mollie. It's still my turn."

She stretched out on the bed, needing fulfillment but wanting this tantalizing lovemaking to continue forever. With careful deliberation, he lowered her shorts. His kisses started at her belly button, then went lower and lower. Flynn kissed every inch of flesh that he bared. His tongue caressed her, driving her crazy. Then he peeled her shorts away.

For a moment, he paused above her, gazing at her pale naked body. The appreciation in his eyes sparked an answer within her. Mollie held her arms wide, welcoming him.

"From the first time I saw you," he said, "I've wanted you."

"For two months?"

"It feels like an eternity. And now, I'm going to make up for lost time."

His tongue teased the shell-like ridges of her ear and descended to the hollow of her throat. His fingers splayed across her breast, down her stomach and reached the triangle of hair at the juncture of her thighs.

When her lips parted in a gasp, his mouth closed over hers, consuming her with a hot but gentle kiss while his hand covered the sensitive flesh between her legs. With slow, exquisite delicacy, he manipulated the intimate folds. His fingers circled lightly and a buzzing electrified her entire body. Her thighs parted.

While his tongue penetrated her mouth, his finger slid inside her, moistening her with tender strokes. Mollie was dizzy with pleasure and she turned her head away from him. "No more, Flynn. I can't wait. I want you. Now."

"But it's still my turn," he whispered.

His finger withdrew, and he changed position. His legs encircled hers, forcing her thighs tightly together. One more light taste of his lips, and his attention lowered to her breasts. His tongue and teeth suckled at her nipples.

Mollie writhed beneath him. Arching and straining. Against her tightly closed thighs, she felt his erection, still shielded from her by his shorts. An incredible orgasmic shuddering went through her. For an instant, she was overwhelmed by sensation. She lost all awareness of where she was and what was happening. And when she came back to earth, Flynn was beside her, holding her, fondling her, teasing her body to new heights.

Impatiently, she tore off his shirt and threw it across the room. Her fingers clawed at his shorts, nearly ripping the waistband.

"I'll do it, Mollie."

"Do it now."

He left the bed, stripped and stood before her, magnificently naked.

Mollie knelt in the center of the bed, admiring his masculine body, which was extremely ready for lovemaking. When he took a small package and sheathed his erection with a condom, she appreciated him even more.

With feline grace, she entered the circle of his arms. The meeting of their warm flesh was sensual and right. She reveled in the texture of the hair on his chest. Her hands possessively stroked the bunches of muscles in his arms and on his back.

"Now, Flynn," she said. "Take me now."

He gazed into her eyes with a look that could only be described as smoldering. When they kissed, an intense heat kindled her desire to an all-conquering blaze. For that moment, nothing else mattered except the arousal they fueled and shared. She spread her thighs and guided him inside her.

With a firm thrust, he entered her slick feminine core. She bucked against him. Their rhythm was slow and sure. Perfectly matched. Mollie was aware that they were both breathing hard. She clung to him, trembling with pleasure, and he stilled his movement.

In that instant of poised tension, he rolled to his back, still within her. With strong hands, he rocked her buttocks against him.

Mollie gasped. The new position surprised and aroused her anew. Her excitement soared as she accepted and answered his thrusts. She was astride him, driven to a nearly frenzied motion. Her hips rotated fiercely. Her entire body quivered with vulnerable, wonderful sensations.

She looked down at his rugged face. His jaw clenched. His eyes squeezed shut.

Their final gasps came simultaneously. Joined together. Complete in their lovemaking. His features relaxed in utter contentment. And Mollie collapsed on his chest, happily exhausted.

She snuggled up against him, at peace with the world, and allowed him to adjust the sheets and covers around them. No matter what happened tomorrow, tonight had been well worth it.

Before she was thoroughly aware of what she was doing, Mollie hummed the little nonsense tune.

"None of that," Flynn said. "We'll search tomorrow."

She sighed. No new words or verses appeared in her mind. No brilliant insights as a result of lovemaking. But she sensed that tomorrow the map would be found in her father's dilapidated hacienda. In the ruins, she thought. Because that was all that was left of her past. Ruins.

"He was an alcoholic," she said softly.

Flynn murmured an assent.

"And alcoholism is supposed to be a disease, like cancer. My father was powerless against it."

"That's the way I understand it, too."

"So, why can't I forgive him? Why am I still so angry and hurt?"

"Relax." He kissed her forehead. "Straightening out your life might take longer than a weekend."

"But I don't have very much time. I need to get my past settled so you and I can . . ." Her voice trailed away. She wanted to make some kind of commitment, but that truly wasn't possible. "Maybe we should make love again."

"What were you saying before? About settling your past?"

"It's not important."

"Yes, Mollie. Your thoughts and emotions are very important to me."

"What about my body?"

"I want to make love to every part of you. Your body and your beautiful mind."

"If we take care of the body, I'll bet that the mind will eventually come around."

When she kissed him, Flynn succumbed to that illogic. His unanswered questions faded as they snuggled together in the cozy sleeping cabin of the fishing boat. The rocking of the waves inspired them to a sensuous new rhythm.

When finally Mollie slumbered in his arms, her relaxation was perfect.

MOLLIE WOKE with the rising sun. Though she could not remember her dreams, she felt driven by a vision that was just beyond her reach. *The Key?* She dropped an affectionate kiss on Flynn's unshaven cheek and crept from the cabin.

As she stepped onto the deck, she saw the roof of her father's hacienda jutting above the palms. And in that moment, she knew where the secret was hidden.

12

MOLLIE RACED TO THE HELM and started the boat's engine. She had to get to shore fast. Though she knew the hiding place, her idea was ephemeral, likely to fade. But she knew! With every fiber of her being, she knew that the answer was there, on shore, right before her eyes.

The engine coughed and sputtered. Anchor, she remembered. She had to weigh anchor. And turn off the running lights.

"Flynn," she shouted. "Flynn, help me."

He stumbled up onto deck, shirtless and blinking at the dawn. "What the hell are you doing?"

"I know where it is." She ran to him, her robe flying around her. "We have to get to shore."

He rubbed his eyes, uncomprehending.

"We have to hurry. It's not a clear memory, just a flicker in the corner of my mind. Hurry."

Flynn was immediately alert. "Go below, Mollie. Get dressed. I'll take us to the pier."

She flew down the metal ladder to below deck and grabbed a pair of shorts and a T-shirt from her suitcase. She could see it in her mind. Wrapped in heavy plastic, the way she'd learned to do when she and her cousins found the cave in Colorado. Not inside the house. But near. It was . . .

She shook herself. It was . . . where?

"Damn."

Mollie dressed, jammed her feet into sneakers and chased back to the helm just as Flynn snugged the fishing boat into the space beside the pier. Her memories were . . . lost.

He turned off the engine and climbed down to moor the boat. "Come on, Mollie."

"It's too late." Her voice shook. "I've forgotten."

"You'll remember again. I'll help you."

Cursing the mists that shrouded her mind, Mollie dragged herself off the boat and joined him on the pier. "Somewhere on Stamper Key, but I don't know where. It's fuzzy now. I must have dreamed about it and still have been half-asleep when I came up on deck."

"Was it the manuscript?"

She nodded. "It was a book, wrapped in heavy plastic."

"What kind of book? How big? Loose pages? A binder? Think, Mollie."

She closed her eyes, tried to think. But her mind was empty of vision, her dream forgotten. "It's gone."

"In the house?" he urged.

"Maybe, but I don't think so."

"Then, where? Dammit."

She startled at the harsh tone in his voice. "Don't be angry. I'm trying as hard as I can to remember."

Flynn strode down the short pier. Away from her. His sneakers thumped against the wooden planks. Though still shirtless, his posture was not casual. She saw tension in the knotted muscles of his back.

Then he pivoted and came back toward her. His jaw thrust forward. "This is one helluva way to wake up. But I'm trying to be patient."

"I didn't do it on purpose."

He glared. With a snap of his head, he went past her and onto the boat.

"Flynn? Where are you going?"

"Marianna gave me the key to the house. We'll start searching in there."

"I don't know if it's there," she warned. "I can't remember."

"Forget remembering. We're going to do this the easy way for a change. There's a possibility that the manuscript is in the hacienda. Or a clue. Or a map. Or a latitude and longitude notation. I plan to take the damn house apart board by board until I find it."

Frustrated, Mollie sank down onto the deck and allowed her head to droop forward. Her hair tumbled around her eyes, obscuring her vision. In her lap, her fingers squeezed into useless fists. She'd been so close to remembering. She'd actually seen a book wrapped in heavy protective plastic.

To be so close. And yet so far away. In her dream, she could have touched the slick plastic covering.

Flynn had returned. His hands slipped beneath her arms and boosted her to her feet like a sack of potatoes. When she gazed into his eyes, she saw no remnant of the love they'd shared the night before. He was cold and distant. Still, she reached toward him, needing him.

When her hands touched his chest, he flinched slightly. Her arms encircled him, and she felt his restraint. Could this be the same man who'd made passionate love to her last night? Of course, he was. But today was the morning after. He didn't have to be sweet to her anymore; he'd gotten what he wanted.

Her opinion wasn't important to him. *The Key* was all that counted. He wanted the missing manuscript, and he was using her to find it. But hadn't she known that from the start?

She pushed away from him. "You'd better not start taking this house apart. If you do, you're no better than a vandal. No better than Rafael Escobar."

"I never claimed to be better than Rafael. This isn't my first time in the Keys, and I've—"

"I should have known. This place would be a magnet to a renegade like you."

"I was here legitimately," he protested.

"Doing what?"

"Exploring a shipwreck for salvage."

"Pirating a ship," she corrected. "And was that before or after you rode bareback on a dolphin, sailed through a hurricane, wrote a book and made love to twenty-two women?"

"After."

"You macho men disgust me." She pivoted and marched along the single-file path past the boat house toward the hacienda.

His exasperated sigh impaled her heart and confirmed her worst fears. Her first instinct had been to mistrust him, and she'd been correct. She never should have allowed herself to be taken in. Though, she had to admit, he had not lied. Flynn had not tried to sweet-talk her into his bed. He had not told her that he loved her.

"Do you have any ideas?" he asked. "Where do we start?"

"Don't worry, I want to find the damn thing as much as you do." Her feeling of betrayal compelled her to add, "Then I can be rid of you and your demands."

"What's that supposed to mean?"

She hurried through the overgrown courtyard with the sundial, not daring to look at him. "I want this treasure hunt to be over so I can get back to my real life."

At the side of the house, he caught her arm. "Mollie?"

She yanked away. "Leave me alone."

"I can't leave you alone. I care about what happens to you."

"Oh, please. Don't start lying to me now." She circled to the front of the house and whipped around. "I've done what you wanted. What gives you the right to be angry at me?"

"I have every damn right." He slammed his fist against the side of the hacienda. "I spent two months convincing you to come on this hunt. I arranged the financing. I kissed off my publisher, and now I've got Edleman breathing down my neck."

He strode away from her, reining his temper, then turned abruptly back to her, nearly trampling a quick green lizard that flitted through the weeds.

This wasn't the way he'd pictured this morning. He'd envisioned a leisurely dawn, making love in the light of day, holding her. He hadn't wanted to fight. It almost seemed as if she were deliberately provoking him, driving him away.

When he gazed at her—with her hair disheveled and her eyes burning with fire—he wanted to make love to this magnificent woman. Not to argue. "Why are you doing this?"

"I'm trying to help. As you cleverly mentioned, Edleman is moving in. And Rafael Escobar will probably be here at any moment with a merry band of scavengers."

"Damn." He kicked at a weed. "Why did your father hide *The Key* in the first place?"

"He was paranoid," she shouted. "I've told you that about ten thousand times. I remember one time, right back here on the patio, my father fired a cook whose name was Wendy. She wore a red dress and a gold heart locket and she was crying. My father was stern and he said, 'Your tears don't fool me. I know you've come to spy for Hitler.' This was during the sixties."

Flynn stared at her. "That's a pretty detailed memory. Do you realize how clearly you remembered that?"

"So what?"

"Maybe your memory block is fading." He took a step toward her. "You might have found your past."

"What if I don't want it? What if I'd rather have the bland memories of an average kid?"

"Not possible. You're far from average. And that has nothing to do with your parentage. You're special, Mollie."

"Great. I don't need this kind of specialness."

She leaned her back against the peeling paint on the house and allowed the morning sun to shine full on her face. She was hurt and angry. In pain. Her emotions were as tangled as the wild flowers and weeds surrounding her father's hacienda. Of course, she wanted her memories. But she feared them, too.

Mollie closed her eyes and allowed an idea to form in her mind. The shape of a book, wrapped in plastic. In a dark place. And yet, there was a flutter of wings. Was it an eagle? A frigate bird? There was sunlight. In her mind, the sky overhead turned green with leaves.

In a flash, she remembered. "The tree house."

She ran to the old dead oak that stood in front of the hacienda. Stripped of its leaves, the dark branches clawed at the sky, and she saw the plywood remains of her childhood tree house. There was a niche up there, a hole in the tree where she'd hidden her treasures.

Mollie grasped a low-hanging branch and began to climb. "It's up here. A book wrapped in plastic."

"Be careful, Mollie. The tree looks rotten."

Balancing carefully, twelve feet off the ground, she neared the tree house. Long ago, when the tree was green with leaves, she'd hidden up here in her secret place, watching the comings and goings of people below.

She'd seen her mother sunbathing—her beautiful mother in a tasteful black swimsuit. And Marianna, bustling through the yard, carrying food. And her father.

In Mollie's memories, the hacienda was restored to its former glory. The hanging baskets of azaleas brought color to the handsome porch. The fresh white paint gleamed in the sunlight.

She boosted herself up the last few feet and crouched on the rotten plywood floor. A chunk of wood gave way beneath her, and she braced her feet on thick branches below the plywood. At eye level, Mollie saw a fat board hung by a single spike, covering the hole in the tree she'd used as a cache. She tried to swing the board out of the way, as she had when she was a child. But the spike had rusted and the board held tightly in place.

"I need a hammer," she called down to Flynn. "Or a crowbar."

Watching from above, she saw him run to the porch of the house. His real figure meshed with her memories—the past clashing with the present.

He grabbed a loose board from the porch and held it up. "Will this do?"

"I'll try it."

Flynn climbed the tree and passed the board to her.

While Mollie struggled to use the board as a lever, he found a vantage point beside her. She broke a fingernail. "I can't budge it."

"May I try?"

"Sure." She edged out of his way. "Behind that board is a cubbyhole where I used to hide things when I was a kid."

Using his bare hands, Flynn pried the board loose.

The hole was revealed—a large, hollow space inside the tree. The edges were smooth but damp.

Normally she wouldn't dare feel around in a rotted tree in a land where lizards and weird bugs abounded. But this was different. She thrust her hand inside and felt something soft and lumpy. Her fingers instinctively recoiled. That thing was certainly not a manuscript. "Yuck, I don't know what this is, but it feels disgusting."

"Do you want me to get it?" Flynn asked.

She shook her head. These were her slimy memories. It was appropriate for her to bring them to light. Gritting her teeth, she reached inside and pulled out a chamois bag. She opened the drawstring to reveal twenty or thirty marbles. Mollie laughed. "My treasures."

There was also a brooch and a garish costume-jewelry necklace, both carefully wrapped in cotton cloth. Then Mollie reached lower into the cubbyhole and felt slick plastic.

"This is it," she said. "I've got it!"

Maneuvering against the inside of the tree, she pulled out a book, sealed against the damp with a heavy plastic. But the shape of it was wrong for a manuscript. This was a small fat book. Mollie tore off the plastic and ran her fingers across the gold lettering on the worn volume.

"'My Diary.'" She read the words with wonderment and delight. "I knew from my dream that there was a secret, but it was my own personal secrets calling to me. Nothing to do with *The Key*."

Mollie opened the first page and studied the childish scrawl across a lined yellowed page. "Today, I am nine," she read out loud, then shook her head and looked away. "Was I ever this young?"

"We all were that young. Full of dreams and secrets." He reached across the tree trunk, caught her hand and squeezed it. "You've made a precious discovery, Mollie."

"My diary? The ramblings of a preadolescent?" She turned to the last page and mentally calculated the date. "The last entry is when I was twelve."

"Three years of Mollie Locke. This should help you find some of your memories."

"But it's probably worthless in terms of locating the manuscript." She met his gaze. "Unless I made a note in here about it."

"We'll study it," Flynn agreed. "But for now, may I help you down from the tree?"

They reached the ground without incident as Mollie clutched the diary to her breast. She was anxious to begin reading, to become acquainted with her childhood as she had recorded it. Not photographs. Not reminiscences from Marscel or her uncle or Marianna. The diary was her very own commentary on a time she'd forgotten.

Despite her eagerness to read, she asked Flynn, "Do you still think we should search the house?"

"Not until I've had coffee."

When they returned to the fishing boat, Flynn went below to prepare breakfast while Mollie stayed on deck with her diary. She flipped the pages at random, noting the dates and discovering that she'd followed an irregular entry system. Some weeks were faithfully recorded, day by day. Often she'd skip a month.

Some pages included lists: "Wash hair. Make bed. Eat breakfast."

And there were brief references to world headlines: "Men walked on the moon—a giant step for mankind. Students got killed at Kent State in a Vietnam war protest. The Beatles broke up, but I still love Ringo."

Flynn returned to the deck, carrying a tray with mugs of coffee and plates of scrambled eggs mixed with cheese and peppers. And conch fritters that Marianna had packed for them.

"Have you found anything interesting?" he asked.

"I had a favorite cat named Lola." She picked up her fork and dug into the eggs. "Strange. I can hardly remember her."

He studied her intently. She seemed distant and somehow out of sync. Not angry, he decided. In fact, she seemed almost without emotion.

In contrast, his own passions were exploding like grenades in his brain. Desire. Anger. Fear. And a caring that was near to love.

His inability to help her frustrated him. He wanted to tell her to forget the damned treasure hunt. To look at him as a man, not a biographer. To burn these complications like so many useless bridges.

He desired her. Spending time with her excited him. Her wit, her intelligence and her depth. He wanted to explore every nuance. And that scared him. Never, in his thirty-five years, had he so strongly wanted to make a commitment. He couldn't imagine being without Mollie.

"When this is over," he said, "I want to spend time with you."

"Let's wait until then before we discuss it."

He set his plate aside and sipped his coffee. "Then, I guess we spend today going through your diary."

"We?" She shook her head. "Not a chance. This is private. Not to mention that it's embarrassing to see what a weird kid I was. I'll read the diary. All by myself, thank you. I promise to tell you if I find a reference to *The Key* or any odd notes about longitude and latitude."

"Should we search the house first?"

"If you want, we can. But I'd really rather reacquaint myself with the diary first. There might be some very obvious clue. Any indication that would give us a direction and save some time."

He glanced toward the hacienda. "I know what you mean. I'm not real excited about digging through the mess in there."

"That'll have to be our last resort," Mollie said. "Marscel and I went through it pretty thoroughly years ago. It seems doubtful that we'll find anything after all this time."

While she settled back to read, Flynn went below and cleaned up the kitchen. He made the bed in the sleeping cabin, tidied up clothes and checked his wristwatch. It was only ten o'clock in the morning.

Back on deck, he puttered, occasionally glancing at Mollie. She'd stretched out on her stomach on a towel and her eyes were glued to the diary. He liked the disarray of her hair as she tucked loose strands behind her ears. The way she unconsciously crossed and uncrossed her bare ankles enticed him.

The fishing boat suddenly seemed too small. Mollie's presence invaded every inch. He needed to touch her, to kiss her. His gaze combed the downy hair on her arms, her delicate wrists and hands. "Would you like some suntan lotion?"

"No, thank you," she replied distractedly.

"Something to drink?"

"No."

"What about—"

"Flynn, I'm fine." She looked up from the diary. "Should I stop reading?"

"I guess not," he said, resigned. "I'm going ashore. In case Rafael or any other scavengers show up."

"Fine."

"And I'd like to get to a phone sometime today. I ought to call my editor and find out why Edleman is snooping around."

"Back to Marianna's?"

"Key Largo is closer. And I used to know a guy there."

"Suit yourself, Flynn."

AFTER A COUPLE OF HOURS exploring the grounds and the boat house and poking around near the base of the sundial, Flynn realized how much he'd depended upon Mollie to lead their search. His own attempts seemed feeble and boring. Get used to it, he told himself. Mollie wasn't going to be around forever.

When Rafael pulled up, driving the car Flynn had rented in Miami, it was almost a relief. The pirates in the Keys had the reputation of playing tough and fighting dirty, but Flynn was ready for some kind of action, some kind of challenge where there were clear winners and losers. "Hello, Rafael."

"Howdy, cowboy." Two other men climbed from the car. "Meet my cousins."

When he saw that all three men were carrying crow-
bars, a cold smile twitched the corner of Flynn's mouth.
He would welcome the chance to beat something or
someone into a pulp. "Why are you here?"

"We thought you might need a hand with your treasure."

"I don't need help."

Flynn braced himself as the taller of Rafael's cousins
approached him. "I think you already found it," he said.

"What if I did?"

"We'll take half." He nodded to Rafael and the other
cousin. "That's fair, huh?"

Rafael shook his head. "No. That ain't right. Marianna would break our . . ." He rattled off a commentary
in rapid Spanish, and the other two cousins backed off.
Rafael turned to Flynn. "I told them you're looking for a
book, and it's not going to make any money for us. No
way."

"Then, I repeat, why are you here?"

"Protection." He spread his hands wide. "You got another call from that Edleman. He's in Miami. So, I figure, you and Miss Locke need somebody to keep an eye
on the place. Huh?"

Not a bad idea, Flynn thought. If the Escobar cousins
were watching the house, he could take off for Key Largo
and call in to his publisher. Plus, their presence might
insure that no other looters arrived.

He draped an arm around Rafael's shoulder. "Here's
the deal. You watch the house. You can go inside and
search—on the condition that you don't tear anything
up." Flynn took his last one-hundred-dollar bill from his
wallet, kissed it and tore it in half. "You get the other
piece when this is over."

Rafael accepted. "But only for one day, Flynn. Hundred bucks a day. That's what we charge."

Flynn left them opening the trunk and taking out a case of beer. Still, he was glad for their protection. Hiring the Escobar cousins was money well spent.

Back on board the fishing boat, he hurried to Mollie's side. "Did you find anything?"

"Nothing." But when she looked up at him, her eyes were filled with pain.

"Do you want to talk."

"No." She turned back to the diary.

"I'm here if you need me. And we're going to Key Largo."

Flynn went to the helm, relieved to have a destination. He needed to be active. The pleasure of swooping across the clear aqua waters immediately soothed him.

Near Key Largo, Flynn paid sharp attention to the many regulations and other boaters. Key Largo was the nearest key to the Florida mainland, the starting point for many charter boats and scuba tours. Finding a space to dock should have been a problem, but Flynn radioed ahead to his old sailing buddy, Jackie Samson, who ran a glass-bottom boat operation. Luckily Jackie was still in business and welcomed Flynn to dock at his pier.

After some pretty fancy maneuvering of the old fishing boat, Flynn turned off the engines and sauntered over to Mollie.

"We're here," he said. "All ashore that's going ashore."

"I'd rather stay here and read."

"Any new revelations?"

"I've just gotten through age nine, and learned that I caught a hammerhead shark on a fishing expedition to the Dry Tortugas." She sat up and looked at him. "I'm ashamed to admit that it's taking forever to decipher some of my scribbly handwriting."

He nodded encouragingly. "Anything about *The Key*?"

"Not a word. However, I was—at nine and a half— quite convinced that I ought to be a writer like my father. Of course, I expected to write about far more important subjects—like outer space."

Her calm revelations gave him the hope that perhaps she would find peace in her childhood, as well as the unhappiness she'd already encountered. "Take a break and come ashore with me. I want you to meet Jackie."

"Who?"

"We're docked at his pier. Jackie Samson. I met him years ago in the Bahamas. He runs a glass-bottom boat operation here in Key Largo."

"Thanks, Flynn. Maybe later?"

He started to object, thought of at least a hundred valid reasons why she should come with him. But he swallowed them all. Flynn knew that he selfishly wanted the pleasure of her company. It was better to give her the space she needed. "Okay, I'll be back in an hour."

"Take your time."

She waved from the deck and watched his tall figure strolling down the pier toward the tourist and diving shops that made up Key Largo. With a small sigh, Mollie settled down to read.

She'd gone well past her tenth birthday before she encountered a strange notation in the diary, "Does alcohol burn like propane?"

Was it a code of some sort? Mollie frowned. A series of memories washed up on the shores of her conscious. Propane was the fuel used for the stove on her father's boat. And she'd associated a lesson from science class with the idea that alcohol has flammable properties.

No clue. Just a simple childhood logic.

And yet, before she turned the page, she knew there was a deeper implication. She read the word *alcohol* over. The round childish script looked so innocent—utterly incongruent with her jaded adult perception. Alcohol meant booze. Vodka, she thought. And gin.

With coral-sharp clarity, she remembered when she'd asked her father that question, does alcohol burn like propane?

They were at the dinner table, the same table that now resided in Marianna's home. Her father was not eating but was drinking instead. He'd been angry at her question, had thought she was accusing him of drinking too much or being dangerously inflammable. His speech had slurred as he told her, "You're the kid. I'm the grown-up. You don't tell me what to do, Mollie."

Then he had laughed and laughed as she sat stiff as a stick at the dinner table. He had raised his glass in toast to her. Very clearly she remembered him saying, "I love you, Green Eyes. Always remember that I love you."

Indeed? She stared at Key Largo from the deck of the fishing boat. Her father loved her so much that he couldn't stay sober. So much that she had to drag him into bed and tuck the covers under his chin. So much that he forgot every promise. And trampled every dream.

Mollie bolted to her feet. She hefted the diary in her hand, ready to fling the book into the sea. If it was possible to drown her memories, she would have done it. But she knew they were inescapable. No matter how she tried to submerge them, they bobbed to the surface like ugly bits of flotsam.

Besides, she thought bitterly, the diary might hold a clue to the location of *The Key*. Flynn would be furious if she lost that chance, no matter how slim it was. Flynn wanted to find the missing manuscript, to make his reputation. And she was the only person who could do that for him.

But why should she?

Tucking the diary under her arm, Mollie left the boat and stalked down the pier. She'd be smart to leave Flynn here—to desert him before she got any deeper.

Under a giant sign advertising glass-bottom boats, she saw a darkly tanned man wearing a captain's hat. He waved and called out, "Yo, it's Mollie, isn't it?"

She waved back, but kept walking briskly, as if she knew where she was going. Home? She wished she'd never left. Her anxiety attacks were nothing compared to the core of rage she'd touched in Central Park. Where was her home? Chicago. Manhattan. How strange that Manhattan had wakened no remembrance of Sergei. For years she had thought he was a grand passion and a tragic disappointment. But their love affair was nothing. And Flynn? Would it be the same with Flynn?

Without destination, Mollie wandered the side streets. Tacky tourist attractions offered seashells that gleamed unnaturally bright and nets that would hold no catch and sale signs offering promises that could never be fulfilled.

Had she been a fool? Mollie stepped up her pace. One memory ached more painfully than the rest. It was not a remembrance of her distant past but only last night. She should have known better than to make love to Flynn. Nothing could come of it. Nothing but pain.

As far as she was concerned, this treasure hunt was over.

13

IN A BEACHFRONT BARROOM, Flynn snuggled the telephone receiver to his ear and listened hard to the voice of his editor. She seemed to be telling him that all was forgiven.

"What about Edleman?" he said. "Why is Edleman in Miami?"

"He offered to act as a liaison. You're both professors. You both have an abiding interest in Woodrow Locke. I thought he might be able to find you and talk some sense into you about your work on the biography."

"Talk sense?"

"You have to buckle down and get serious, Flynn."

While she continued to offer calm, rational explanations, Flynn made his own deduction: his editor had decided that he was not reliable, and Edleman was making a bid to take his place.

Flynn's reasoning went a step farther. Having someone else write the biography wasn't a bad idea. Since he had come to know Mollie, his perspective on the renowned Woodrow Locke had changed considerably. He wasn't sure that he could write an objective portrait.

Someone plugged a coin into the barroom jukebox, and his editor's sane comments were garbled by the competing noise.

"How do I find Edleman?" he shouted into the telephone.

"Tell me where you are," she said. "He'll find you. The man is nothing if not persistent."

Flynn gave the location of Jackie's Glass-Bottom Boat Tours, promised to keep in touch and rang off.

In four long strides, Flynn was at the bar, ordering a beer and wondering if he'd completely lost his mind. Give up the biography? Was he actually considering the possibility of giving up the honor and the challenge? Of allowing someone else to write the first authorized biography of Woodrow Locke? Marscel would kill him. Flynn's academic reputation would be shot. His editor would not be amused.

But Mollie would be glad. If the biography wasn't standing between them, if she had no reason to believe he was using her, it was possible for them to have a future together. Flynn took a long swallow of the beer and frowned. Mollie's approval or disapproval was not a sound basis for making professional decisions.

While the jukebox played a mournful tune about losing in love, he stared across the bar at the glittering rows of bottles. Never in his life had Flynn perched on a bar stool, worrying about what a lady would think, and it didn't make sense to start now. Especially not when the lady was only a few blocks away.

He left the half-finished beer and headed back to her. A few quick stops and he'd purchased shrimp, fresh bread, kiwi, juice . . . and a dozen red roses.

At the harbor, he still felt off balance. Mollie hadn't asked him to give up the biography. Or the search for *The Key*. Yet he couldn't escape the truth that he had used her memories on this treasure hunt.

He hated to think of himself that way. A user. He stared beyond the azure waters, the gleaming white masts and the wistful dream of a sky. The sea rhythms should have soothed him. The gulf breeze that danced through feathery coconut palms should have swept confusion from his mind.

Find *The Key*, he told himself. Write the biography. Move on with life.

Instead, he stood on the pier and visualized Mollie traveling with him across this sea. Or to the Arctic Ocean, the Caribbean, the Mediterranean. They would sail together, fly together, and she would never be burdensome or touristy. Her eclectic childhood had prepared her to share his adventures. She was already a world traveler, not easily impressed. Her appreciation would have greater depth; she could even teach Flynn a thing or two.

Yet she was also innately, touchingly sensitive. She might be cool, but she wasn't tough. He knew the lost little girl who lived within her.

Striding through the harbor, he faced the fact that she was the perfect woman for him. By the time he reached the old fishing boat, he was ready to dash on board and ask Mollie if she would live with him. And equally prepared to run like hell if she said that she would.

He boarded the boat at half past one. Mollie was not on deck.

He climbed below, "Mollie? Where are you?"

Dumping his parcels onto the small kitchen table, he went into the sleeping cabin. She wasn't there. He searched the boat thoroughly. She was nowhere.

His heartbeat accelerated. A panicky feeling boiled up in his chest as he stood on deck, scanning in all directions. Had he made his decision too late? Had she left him?

Flynn ordered himself to calm down. Mollie was an adult, he reasoned, a sensible woman who wouldn't just disappear. More than likely, she'd gone to find something to eat. She'd be back in a minute. He settled uneasily to wait. But the minutes trickled past like the slow drip of a leaky faucet. By two o'clock, he couldn't stand it anymore.

He jogged down the pier to the shanty where Jackie Samson sat, tipped back in his chair and whittling. Jackie raised his knife in salute. "Yo, buddy."

"Hey, Jackie. Have you seen the lady who came with me?"

"You bet." He nodded. "You always were a leg man."

"Which way did she go?"

Jackie held up the piece of wood he was shaping with his knife and studied the emerging form of a dolphin in midleap.

"Which way?" Flynn repeated.

"You sound tense, buddy. Is this the lady who's finally going to put a crimp in your air hose and make you settle down?"

Was she? "This is a business trip."

"Business, eh?" A knowing grin creased Jackie's weathered face. "Oh, yeah, you've got it bad, buddy. Lovesick worse than the bends. Hey, I got some oxygen in the back if you think you're close to hyperventilating."

"Just tell me where she went."

He pointed toward the east. "Am I invited to the wedding?"

"No plans like that," Flynn grumbled. "But keep the oxygen handy."

Though Flynn kept his pace to a saunter, his eyes searched in every direction, peering into every face. Where was she? He stalked the streets of Key Largo, looking into shops and cafés. What if something had happened to her? Should he contact the police? No, that would be a useless exercise. They'd only laugh when he complained that his attractive female companion had wandered off. Key Largo was only a few square miles in size. But what if she'd taken off toward Pennekamp park? Taken up scuba diving? A small aircraft buzzed overhead. In the sky? She could be anywhere.

At the beach, he walked slowly. There was such a thick crowd that he could never spy Mollie here. And yet he figured this was the most likely place. Mollie liked crowds. He scanned the tanning throng—teenagers in minuscule swimsuits, small brown children who splashed in the warm water near the shore, sensible mothers under umbrellas. No Mollie.

What if she'd gone home to Chicago? Or what if she'd found the clue and was, at this very moment, discovering *The Key*? But Mollie wouldn't do either of those things. She was ultraconscious of her responsibilities. It was unthinkable that she would have undertaken a major change of direction without notifying him.

Something must have happened to detain her. Swallowing his pride, Flynn returned to the barroom and used the telephone to contact the hospitals, the coast guard and the police. There had been no accidents or arrests that involved a woman who looked like Mollie.

He slammed down the receiver. Maybe she'd left a note on the boat, and he hadn't seen it. Flynn returned to the fishing boat. And found nothing.

He stood on deck, staring at the warm tropical sea and the sky. Where in the hell was she?

By four o'clock, Flynn was pacing the deck. It wasn't the best time in the world for delicate negotiations with Edleman. But that was who Flynn spied, strolling up the pier.

"A fine coincidence," Edleman said. "Hello, Flynn."

"I can't talk right now."

"How's Mollie?"

Though Flynn tried to remain expressionless, Edleman read him like a book.

"Dear me." Professor Edleman feigned shock. "Have you two had a spat? Perhaps I should offer comfort to the fair Miss Locke?"

"Mollie's not here." And there wasn't much Flynn could do about that now. He sat cross-legged on the deck, took a deep breath and said, "All right, Edleman. You've found me. Now, state your proposition."

"Frankly, my dear colleague, you've just about blown your chances at the biography. You've missed deadlines and been difficult. That might be acceptable for a writer of suspense novels—" his tone clearly placed suspense novels a step beneath laundry lists "—but not for scholarly, well-researched endeavors."

"So, you're offering to get me off the hook. To take over the biography for me."

"In a word, yes."

"Why bother talking to me? Even if I agree, you'd still have to get past Marscel."

"Not exactly. The contracts with the publishing house would override Marscel's veto. We'd share credit on the cover."

While Edleman panted after the opportunity, Flynn surprised himself once again by giving serious weight to Edleman's offer. If he turned over the writing of the biography to this jerk, Mollie would believe—once and for all—that he wasn't using her. And it would solve his dilemma about his own newly negative opinion of Woodrow Locke.

But there was a down side. If Flynn backed out, he would destroy John Marscel's dream of a true biography. And Edleman would be pestering Mollie for interviews, raking her past up again. "Could you leave Mollie out of it? No interviews?"

"None should be necessary."

Flynn had never been a quitter. But this decision was more complicated than facing the last hundred feet of a mountain climb. If he quit, he could have Mollie. She'd understand his sacrifice. She'd appreciate that he'd chosen her over fame and fortune.

But if he quit, he'd lose his integrity. He wouldn't be Flynn. And if she couldn't accept him for what he was...

"Sorry, Edleman. I can't give it up."

"Of course, I expected some resistance." He reached into his trousers pocket, took out his wallet and produced a check. "I'm prepared to make a substantial financial offer. You see, Flynn, I don't need the money for writing this book. But you do. Your publisher has informed me that you've used up a sizable advance and incurred a debt, as well."

"Money's irrelevant." Flynn shrugged. "When I offer the publishers a completed missing novel from Woodrow Locke, I'll be able to name my price for the biography."

"But *The Key* might not exist. Mollie was rather explicit during that nasty little meeting in New York. And, if I recall correctly, so were you."

"I haven't given up."

"Let me put it this way. Accept my offer right now. Or accept half of the same offer in a month when you've proven that you can't write a biography. And can't find this nebulous manuscript."

"I'm not interested."

Flynn hopped off the boat onto the pier and started walking fast. Edleman followed. "You'd best take my offer now, Flynn. This isn't like one of your macho stunts. You can't force a missing manuscript to reappear."

Abruptly Flynn swung around. "Keep away from me. Keep away from Mollie. I won't see you in a month. Or ever."

"Oh, you'll see me. When you fail to find *The Key*, you'll come begging."

"Go to hell, Edleman."

Flynn moved along the pier in an easy saunter. His sense of resolve had been restored. He knew who he was—a biographer and a writer. If Mollie despised him for that, he'd have to live without her. Because he couldn't change. And he wouldn't quit.

Maybe it was true that he'd started out by using her to gain information. But she'd known that. She'd agreed to it. And their relationship had grown beyond it. Last night they had become one heart. She had cared for him whether or not he was a professor or a writer or a pirate.

Flynn set out to search for her. If he could hope to find a manuscript that had been missing for twenty years, he could surely find one green-eyed woman.

14

WITH TEDIOUS PRECISION, he checked every diving shop and charter boat operation. He went from four-star restaurant to hot dog stand. From shop to shop. He walked the beachfront time and time again.

When the tropical sun hung low in the skies, Flynn stood on the Key Largo beach, digging his heels into the hard white sand and scanning the sunbathers. No Mollie. Had she actually left Key Largo? Left him without a note?

He worked his way through the sun-worshipping throng to the edge of the smooth waves, wishing her return on the next tide. But maybe it was better that she was gone. Sooner or later, they would have to part. Might as well be sooner.

Flynn stripped off his Hawaiian-style shirt and waded far beyond the shore until he was waist deep in water. He cleansed himself, washed away the nervous sweat and splashed back to the beach. And then he heard her voice.

"Flynn, I'm over here."

He saw her. Walking across the white sand toward him and waving. In her hand, she carried the diary.

He dashed to her and scooped her into his arms. Under his breath, Flynn muttered, "Where the hell have you been?"

"Nice to see you, too."

He squeezed her against him. Relief spread over him like a balm. "I've searched every square inch of this island."

"I've been sitting by that palm tree, reading my diary."

He must have passed that tree a dozen times. Why hadn't he seen her?

"I'm sorry," she said. "I should have left a note."

"Damn right, you should have. I've been calling hospitals and the coast guard, imagining the worst."

Yet his justifiable anger shattered into a million pieces when he gazed into her eyes. She looked terribly tired. Though her complexion had a healthy tan and the tip of her nose was pink with sunburn, dark shadows haunted her expression. Her lips were drawn in a straight, expressionless line.

Flynn was solicitous. "Would you like to sit down? Have you had anything to eat or drink?"

"Of course. I'd be dehydrated if I hadn't."

Her arm raised, and she pointed to a cheesy little beachfront stand where soda and snacks could be purchased. Flynn had been there. He'd asked the kid behind the counter if he'd seen a tall brunette with green eyes and had received a negative reply. Then he looked down at Mollie. "You were wearing sunglasses."

She tapped the glasses in her shirt pocket. "Yes. Why?"

He'd spent the entire day searching for a woman with incredible green eyes, asking for a green-eyed brunette, and she'd covered her most dominant feature with dark glasses. A perfect, unplanned disguise.

"What's wrong?" she asked.

"Never mind. If all you've had is junk food, you must be hungry and thirsty," he said. "Let's go back to the boat."

"I truly am sorry for the inconvenience."

"Sounds like something you'd say to a business associate."

"That's what we are."

Her words stung. He didn't feel like an associate or a collaborator or a colleague. He felt like a lover who had ached inside when she was gone. Finding her brought the meaning back into life.

And yet, he'd chosen to continue with the biography rather than to give up everything for her. Maybe he deserved to be treated like a co-worker. He took her arm and led her to the shoreline. "Anything interesting in your diary?"

"There wasn't a thing about the location of the manuscript," she said. "But I found references to *The Key*."

Despite his concern for Mollie, Flynn thought of the biography. Mollie's diary would be a priceless reference. He gritted his teeth, knowing how much she hated sharing her memories and how much she feared seeing them in print. It was better, much better, that they part. "May I see your diary?"

"No. But I'll read to you." Without preamble, she plunked down onto the sand and turned to the latter pages of the small book. "This was when I was eleven. It says: 'Dad was mad today because I talked back. He says I have a nasty temper, and he's going to put that in some stupid book he's writing for me so the whole wide world will know how naughty I am.'"

She flipped to another page and read, "'I hate *The Key*. I wish he'd throw it away. Why couldn't my father be a fireman?'"

Her chin trembled, and Mollie felt a tear slide down her cheek. She'd been crying a lot today. And, strangely, she didn't care, wasn't embarrassed. As she read the diary and became absorbed in her own memories, the mask she presented to the world had slipped. It was as if she didn't care what other people thought of her. Including Flynn. Or especially Flynn. She shouldn't allow herself to care what he thought.

"It's okay," he said. His hand lifted and he caught her tear on his fingertip. "It's all right to feel the way you're feeling."

"Is it?" She glared sharply. "To cry every time I felt like crying? Or shout when I'm angry? I'd be like my father in one of his macho drunken moods when he'd try to pick fights."

"Many people loved your father."

"They excused him," she corrected, "because he was a genius and supposed to be colorful. But they didn't live with him. Have you noticed that lovable Woodrow Locke had a miserable track record with the women who married him?"

"Doesn't matter, Mollie. You're not your father."

"Thank God!"

He took both her hands in his and pulled her upright. He faced her. "Emotional outbursts don't have to be crying and screaming. And you know it. There's laughter, too. And loving, making love."

"Passion? But that has to be controlled, too."

"And it's a good thing. Otherwise, I might throw you down on the sand, right here on this public beach, and ravish your body."

She bent down and scooped up the diary. "Let's go back to the boat."

Hand in hand, they walked silently along the shore. Flynn pointed out the bar where he had used the telephone. Again the jukebox was playing. This time, it was an old Elvis Presley tune.

"The King," Flynn said.

"You're an Elvis fan? I can't imagine an English professor bopping along with old Elvis records."

"Well, I'm not your garden-variety English professor."

"I see." She teased, "So? Is the King still alive?"

"Let's just say that I wouldn't be surprised if Elvis walked out of that bar wearing blue suede shoes."

"Maybe that should be your next biography. You could find Elvis's daughter and try to track him down."

"Not very scholarly, but it's a fascinating thought. Why would someone like Elvis—a world-renowned star—want to disappear?"

"Fame hurts." Self-consciously Mollie hastily added, "Not that I personally know anything about being famous, but it seemed to upset my father. He hated being recognized. But, at the same time, he kind of expected it."

At the pier, Flynn waved to Jackie and shouted, "Found her."

"Good work. Don't let her get away." He waved a piece of paper. "And I got a message for you. From that Edleman guy."

"Edleman?" Mollie questioned sharply. "You saw him?"

"I did. And it wasn't a treat."

He took the note from Jackie and whisked Mollie down the pier. The message said that Edleman's offer was good until midnight and gave a motel where he was staying. Flynn wadded the paper and stuck it into his pocket.

"What about Edleman?" Mollie probed. "What did he want?"

On the deck of the fishing boat, Flynn faced her. "He made me an offer to take over the writing of your father's biography. I considered it. I really thought about it."

"Why?"

"If I gave up the biography, I wouldn't be using you anymore. We would just be two people. Not Woodrow Locke's daughter and his biographer. We could be together." He winced inside. "I'm sorry, Mollie, I couldn't quit. I'm not made that way."

"Of course not." Some of the pain faded from her eyes as she gazed up at him. "I'm glad you didn't."

"You are?"

Flynn would never understand this woman. He'd expected her to slap his face. Instead she glided her arms around his neck.

"I am," she confirmed. "And I'm tremendously complimented that you even considered such a thing."

He placed his hands at her slim waist. "Do you understand? By turning down Edleman's offer, it means that our original agreement stands. When our search is over—and I can only afford a few more days—I'll have to leave you. To get back to Maine and write this biography."

She smiled. "What if we find *The Key*?"

"It would take a lot of the pressure off me. But it wouldn't change anything else. We can't be together while I'm working on this book about your father. I don't want to exploit you."

"But if I'm willing?"

"No. It still wouldn't be right. You'd be afraid to talk to me. And I'd be constantly compromising myself in the biography, trying to second-guess your reactions."

"Well, then." She lightly kissed his lips. "Since tonight might be our last time together, I'd suggest that we don't waste another minute."

He nodded. "Let's cast off. We're going back to Stamper Key."

She busied herself with the business of leaving Key Largo harbor. In moments, they were beyond the sea-going traffic and on their way. Mollie sighed and glanced heavenward. Another beautiful sunset was in the making. These skies would be hers and Flynn's alone. And tonight. Only tonight?

Unfortunately, his reasoning was correct. They couldn't have any sort of relationship if he was in a position to use her. And she'd always been so willing to be used. With grim determination, she pushed that thought from her mind. She peeled off her shirt and shorts, wanting to feel the sea breeze all over her body.

Flynn noticed. "Wow! Where did you get that bathing suit?"

"This old thing?" She smoothed the turquoise maillot. "In Biscayne Bay when I bought all the shirts."

"Wow!" he repeated appreciatively. His gaze traveled the considerable length of her legs, from her well-shaped thighs to the toes of her espadrilles. "Very nice."

"It's a bit too high cut in the legs," she said. "Probably not going to be practical for swimming."

"You look like a mermaid. I've thought that since the first time I saw the green of your eyes."

She felt a warm flush under her tan. A mermaid? She'd never thought of herself as a mysterious siren who was capable of luring men beyond their depth. Especially not a self-possessed man like Flynn. His stance at the wheel was so natural. His strong legs were braced against the rolling of the boat. He was so innately masculine.

"I love this," he said. "The misty spray. The salt water."

"The stink of fish," she reminded.

"That's the smell of life." He turned to her and grinned. "There's one of my memories. My father used to say that every time I went into the barn."

"It's difficult to picture you as a former farm boy."

"Not that different from being a seaman. Farmers and sailors both live with the secure knowledge that the earth will provide for us."

"If we don't destroy it with oil spills and dumping and acid rain and pollution."

"You're right. Please accept my belated apologies for any snide comments I've made about your 'whale saving.'" He bowed in her direction. "I've always trusted so firmly in the earth's bounty that I haven't paid enough attention to preserving it."

"Maybe nobody has."

For the moment, she was content to leave those problems to someone else. She spread a beach towel on the deck. Lying full length on her stomach, she trained her eyes on the west. The sunset was just beginning when Flynn dropped anchor off the shore from Stamper Key.

He went below deck and returned, wearing navy blue swim trunks and carrying two icy glasses of orange juice. He sat beside her and they silently watched the slow spread of crimson.

When the golden sun was swallowed up by the horizon, he joined his mouth with hers. Her rose-tinted flesh was uncommonly sensitive as he stripped away her bathing suit and kissed her breasts. His gentle lovemaking harmonized with the whisper of the sea and his caresses were as fresh as tangy breezes.

He poised above her, gazing fondly, and whispered, "A mermaid. A tantalizing mermaid with alluring green eyes."

Before Mollie could protest that she was only a woman, he entered her. Rhythmic thrusts of sheer pleasure drove objections from her mind.

When their passion had been fulfilled, they lay side by side on the deck of the old fishing boat. Though the skies were not yet dark, it was a dreamy time. Magical.

Flynn sighed. "I need to go ashore and pay off the pirates I hired to watch the hacienda."

"What pirates?"

"Rafael Escobar and his cousins."

Before she could question him further, Flynn had slipped into his swim trunks and dived into the warm Key waters.

On the deck of the fishing boat, Mollie watched the colors fade lazily from the sky. The memory of the sun's warmth glowed on her face. The rustle of breezes through palm fronds and the lapping of the pure blue waters against the hull made a beautiful melody. When Flynn reappeared and climbed onto the boat, she felt content and peaceful inside.

"Good," he said, pulling off his wet swimsuit. "You're still naked."

"Nude and lazy." She lay on her stomach. When he stretched out beside her, she sighed. "I wish I'd found something more useful in my diary. A better clue."

"Don't worry about it."

Though he was wet from his swim, she snuggled against him. "I learned a code while I was reading in the diary."

"A what?"

"A code," she repeated. "'Daddy was sick last night' translates to a drunken binge. The same goes for 'tired,' 'silly,' and 'angry.' The only time he didn't drink was in the morning when he wrote. And I know how he managed that. He'd roll out of bed, gulp down two aspirin and a concoction of egg yolks and hot sauce. I used to make it for him."

Though the air was still warm, Mollie shivered. "There wasn't room for much in his life, except for booze and reams of white paper that he felt compelled to fill with words."

"He wasn't all bad. He must have cared about you."

"I suppose he did. As well as he could."

"I suppose so."

"In some ways, you're like him. A writer. An adventurer." She studied Flynn's rugged features by starlight. "My father was driven by his writing. But what drives you?"

"Curiosity, maybe. I always want to know what's beyond the next wave, what's hidden on the next shore. There's a thrill about finding something new."

"You should have been an explorer, conquering new worlds."

"Perhaps I am." With a fingernail, he traced intricate patterns on her back. "But the continents have been mapped, and the seas have all been sailed." He drew a circle around each cheek of her buttocks. "Lucky for me, there's always another frontier."

"I've never thought of myself as a frontier."

"But you are." He turned her chin toward him. "There's a galaxy in your smile. Your eyes speak of lands more wonderful and dangerous than have ever been charted on a map."

His finger glided down her throat.

"Your breasts," he murmured.

She quivered at his touch. "What about my breasts?"

"Let's just say that I could spend hours exploring the mysteries of your breasts."

"Let's say more than that." She batted her lashes, beaming a Milky Way of desire. "Let's go below to the cabin."

Flynn needed no more encouragement. He led her through the hatchway, down the stairs and through the tiny kitchen, where Mollie paused at the sink.

"Roses? Flynn, they're beautiful." She straightened the bouquet he had carelessly discarded and inhaled its fragrance. Then she began digging through the cabinets. "We have to find something to put them in."

Flynn considered dissuading her, sweeping her off her feet and dragging her to his bed. But he dismissed the thought. She was too determined. Even when naked and ready for lovemaking, Mollie was much too practical to leave roses to wither.

Besides, he thought, watching her was a rare feast. She made a lovely feminine picture as she filled a pitcher with water and arranged the long-stemmed bouquet. Her fingers delicately handled the flowers and avoided the thorns. In a moment, she had created loveliness from a dumped mess of flowers.

"You're incredible," he said. "Absolutely unpredictable. One hundred percent female."

She carried the bouquet into the small sleeping cabin. "Do you think the rocking of the boat will spill it?"

"At this point, I don't much care," he said, flopping down onto the bed. "Come here, Mollie. I haven't got much patience left."

"Nor do I." Gracefully, she arranged herself beside him on the bed. "For somebody who could spend hours exploring my breasts, you certainly are in a hurry."

"We'll go as slowly as you want."

His kiss, however, was not a languid, lazy exploration. His mouth consumed her with a hard, possessive passion. His tongue thrust between her lips, boldly arousing her as his fingers manipulated the flesh of her breast.

With sure awareness, Flynn played the role of aggressor, claiming her body. He lifted her toward him, arching her back, and Mollie was compelled to respond in like manner. She needed Flynn's virility, his unquestioning assurance. She wanted him. And she would have him. His body, his gorgeous male body, was hers for the night.

Her swollen breast filled his palm. Her thighs spread and encircled him. She gave herself entirely, without holding back. Every inch of her body, every fragment of her imagination, was dedicated to sheer sensuality.

The fragrance of roses tingled her nostrils. She heard the waves against the hull and felt the exquisite, hard strength of his erection. When he entered her, Mollie's senses throbbed. She was driven almost out of herself. And then, at last, she was at peace. Utter, beautiful peace.

She lay quietly beside him. Her mind was blank—no thoughts, no memories, no ideas. Flynn held her until, finally, she slept.

The next morning, they took their leisure in redefining the limits of their own sleepy passion with slow, gentle lovemaking. Though they did not match the intensity of the previous night, there was a companionable satisfaction in their nearness.

Afterward Mollie lazily sprawled across the pillows. "Why don't we just spend the next two or three weeks in bed?"

"We don't have that long."

His words sliced through her contentment. Numbly she dressed. They shared coffee, made plans to enter the hacienda and moored the fishing boat at the pontoon pier. It wasn't until they reached the tumbledown porch at the doorstep of her father's hacienda that she objected. "Why, Flynn? Why do you have to leave me?"

"I've got to write the biography. To fulfill my commitment."

"But I could still stay with you. If anybody is accustomed to living with a writer, it's me."

"It wouldn't work. If you stayed with me while I worked on the biography, you'd always suspect I was using you." Gently he stroked a tendril of hair from her forehead. "I can't promise that I wouldn't ask questions, that I wouldn't probe, that your words would not show up in print."

"I don't care."

"When we started this search, we made our plans. I wanted to find *The Key*. You wanted to make peace with your past. When it was over, we knew that we would go back to separate lives."

"Plans can change."

"And I hope they will. When the biography is finished, I hope you'll still want to be with me."

"How long?"

"Six months. Maybe a year." He stepped onto the porch ahead of her. "Let's take this final step, Mollie. The hacienda is our last real hope. If there's nothing here, I doubt that we'll ever find the manuscript." Then, using the key that Marianna had given him, Flynn unlocked the front door.

15

MOLLIE DIDN'T BELIEVE in the supernatural. Yet when the door to her father's hacienda creaked open, a chill slithered down her spine, and she could easily imagine her father as a chain-rattling specter who haunted this desolate place.

Flynn must have felt it, too, because he came down the steps to stand by her side. His attitude, however, indicated that he would be perfectly delighted to meet a ghost. "Weird, huh?"

"I feel like some kind of Gothic heroine in a horror movie who knows there's an ax-wielding weirdo inside the haunted house. I've always wondered why those heroines go inside."

"Because they have brave protectors, like me, to stand by their side."

"Really? Of course, you realize that the so-called protector is usually the first to meet his grisly demise."

"Seriously, Mollie, are you scared?"

"There's no reason to be. Rationally, I know it's nothing but an empty house."

"Not empty." He took her hand. "Unless I miss my guess, it's populated with memories. Your memories."

She squeezed his hand, glad for his presence. By herself, Mollie would have turned and run like hell. Not because of superstition, but because she had a sure sense that this house would be the final confrontation—the place where she would come face-to-face with her past.

Either she would find peace or she would close the door forever. "Okay, Flynn. Let's go."

The porch step groaned when she stepped upon it, and Mollie inadvertently recoiled. She looked up at the hacienda once again. It used to be so pretty. Or maybe not. Maybe it was always like this—moldy and cold with paint peeling and windows broken. Maybe her memory was a facade, like one of those false-front buildings used on Hollywood sets. Maybe she'd imagined the loveliness to hide the inner deterioration.

It was only a house. According to Marscel, it was *her* house. And she'd ignored it for all these years. One foot after the other, she marched forward. She'd come this far and wasn't about to turn back.

When Flynn pushed the front door wide and Mollie saw the foyer, she cringed. The wood floor was warped and dull. Sunlight slanted through the boarded-over windows, casting weird shadows against peeling wallpaper. Twisted wires dangled from the ceiling, marking the place where a brass chandelier had hung.

The graceful curve of the wrought-iron banister leading upstairs contrasted with the other deterioration. Her father had stood at that banister so many times. He'd stumbled down those stairs. She remembered his eyes, bloodshot and burning like dark coals. He'd make an effective ghost, lurching inexorably toward her, clinging to her, holding her against him.

She shook away that vision. "It's not so bad. I'm actually rather amazed that the house is still standing after being abandoned all these years."

"It hasn't been totally empty," Flynn said. "Remember? Marianna told us she had allowed various relatives who were down on their luck to live here."

"That's typical." A nervous laugh bubbled from Mollie's lips. "From shipwrecks to house wrecks, the Escobars won't let anything go to waste."

To the left of the foyer was a parlor. To the right was a guest room. Mollie spared a quick glance at both of those cold empty places, noting with regret the filthy sofa that had once been shiny damask and the cracked mirror over the mantel.

The hallway seemed more narrow than when she was a little girl. The cold walls of the corridor leading toward the rear of the house were claustrophobic. The musty odor of rot was strongest here, inescapable.

The door to her father's office was closed, and Mollie paused with her hand above the glass knob. This had been his lair, the only place where he truly came alive.

Flynn touched her shoulder. "What me to go first?"

"Thank you, but no. These are my monsters."

She turned the knob and walked inside. Though the bookshelves were empty now, her father's office was much the same as it had been when she was a child. Marianna must have concentrated her cleaning forays on this room. The huge oak desk sat squarely on a rattan floor mat. In the corner of the room was a heavy wooden table with a display of cut-glass bottles on a cheap stainless steel tray.

"Is this where he worked?" Flynn asked.

"Please don't get awestricken," she said. "If you start reverently stroking the desk and extolling the works of genius that poured forth from that desk, I swear that I'll throw you through the window."

In this room, the windows were not boarded or shuttered, and the glass was unbroken. "Strange," she said. "Did you notice the windows?"

"It's odd," he agreed. "But the trees are thickest here. They must have provided protection."

"Even with Marianna's family in residence, I can't believe this place hasn't been vandalized."

"It's remote," Flynn pointed out. "I doubt anyone would stumble across Stamper Key unless they were looking for it."

"Why weren't they looking? All my life, I've been pestered by people who were researching my father. Why didn't they come here?" She waved at the bottles on the table. "Why didn't they take his damn booze bottles to use as icons?"

She grabbed one of the cut-glass bottles by the neck. "This was vodka."

When she reached for the gin bottle, a huge black spider scuttled across the table. With a shriek, Mollie jumped and dropped the bottle she was holding. The cut glass smashed on the floor and broke neatly in half, spilling dust.

Flynn was beside her, embracing her. "What, Mollie?"

"Only a spider." But she gripped his forearm with the fierce strength of tension. "I'm all right."

"Talk to me. Tell me about this room. What happened in here?"

"Are you trying to get me talking so I won't be nervous? Like whistling in a graveyard?"

He nodded. "Try it."

She moved away from him and launched into a tour guide spiel. "In this very room, at that very desk, Woodrow Locke would pound away at his manual typewriter, creating his masterpieces. He wakened every morning quite early. He showered and shaved and came here. Woodrow Locke firmly believed that it was important to maintain cleanliness. A slovenly appearance, he said, was the first step on the road to ruin."

"What about you?" Flynn questioned. "What does this room mean to you?"

"His daughter," she said, gesturing grandly to the door, "would often look in while her father was working. If she was early enough, he would nod to her and she would run to the kitchen to fetch his favorite morning antidote for hangover."

"You'd go to the kitchen and fetch his egg yolk drink," Flynn clarified. "Then what would you do?"

"Though Locke seldom acknowledged his daughter's appearance or looked up from his work, she enjoyed being here with him. In this office, she would play quietly in his presence."

She stuttered as her memories raced faster than her words. "Then, what? Sometimes he'd hum when he worked. But I never made a peep. Then, he'd finish his work for the day. And he would reach inside this bottom desk drawer."

With an effort, she yanked the warped drawer open. "It's still here. His last bottle."

Kicking the drawer closed, she stalked away from the desk. "There's no clue in this room, Flynn. Other than the fact that my father was a habitual drinker, there's nothing."

They went through the kitchen with its huge old stove and refrigerator. The sink was grotesquely begrimed. They passed the walk-in pantry where two lizards played among moldy empty shelves and came to a large room encircled by boarded-up windows. Most of the glass had been shattered. "This was the glass house. For people who shouldn't throw stones. I usually played in here."

Mollie's playroom was the most cluttered. Shards of glass littered the floor by the windows. There were four wooden chairs. A couple of cigarette butts. Leftover toys lay in rotting heaps. She recognized the head of a porcelain doll with blue eyes staring blindly. There was a toy box, an upright piano and a shabby sofa bed.

"This stuff must have been too beat-up for Marianna," she said. Gingerly she picked the doll's head from the rubble. "My father bought me this doll," she said. "Her name was Ingrid and she wore an authentic Swedish costume. Quite an expensive toy for a little girl, but he encouraged me to play with her. I can hear him saying, 'Ingrid looks lonely.'"

"Did he ever play dolls with you?"

"Mr. Macho? Are you kidding?" Nonchalantly she tossed the doll's head back into the rubbish pile. "It wasn't by accident that I left lovely Ingrid out in the rain. I wanted to get back at him, to make him pay attention to me. And he did. He was so furious that he ripped the doll's head off. I managed to repair her costume, but the head never fit properly again."

"Was there any game you'd play with him?"

"Hide-and-seek. Isn't that the perfect game for a paranoid person like my father?"

"Was he really? Paranoid?"

"You bet." She stood in the middle of the room, arms akimbo. "That was why he taught me to defend myself—how to jab and counterpunch. Does that seem an unusual skill to teach a girl?"

Flynn considered for a moment before answering, "Not really. I had sisters, and they got into as many scrapes as I did. A knowledge of sparring might have been useful to them."

"I only did it because I thought my father wanted me to be tough. For a while, this room had a punching bag set at my level. He'd hear me in here, smacking at the bag, and he'd come in and watch."

She heard the wistful echo of her father's laughter. "Sometimes, I wish things could have been different between my father and me. If only I could have trusted him. If I hadn't been so angry. If I hadn't felt like his drinking was somehow my fault. Maybe if he hadn't been famous." Her head was spinning. "Maybe if I were somebody else."

"I'm glad you're you." Flynn crossed the room and hugged her against him. "The bravest woman I know. Do you realize that you've succeeded, Mollie?"

"In what?"

"This search for your past. When we started out, you were barely able to acknowledge that your father was an alcoholic. You couldn't recall the sound of his voice."

"Now, I hear him," she said ruefully. "Loud and clear."

"At least you know what's gnawing at you. You can see where the hurt comes from. And the confusion."

Yet the giant strides she'd taken toward understanding herself and her past were small comfort. "Just because I know a cyclone is approaching, I can't make it turn back to sea."

"You'll weather this. You've always had the strength to weather the fear and pain and anger." He hugged her. "You're going to make it."

But what about tomorrow? The future. How could she begin to consider the future? What lay ahead was a whole other problem, another set of fears and doubts. With a mental flip-flop, she saw her past becoming her future. It could be repeated. It might be a cycle.

Though her father was dead, she'd kept him alive in her heart. Though she'd hated him, she'd been searching for him. In her other relationships with men, had she been looking for her father? The thought was almost too terrible to comprehend.

She lifted her chin and looked Flynn in the eye. He wasn't her father, wasn't alcoholic. But he was going to leave her after the manuscript was found. Just like her father, Flynn would abandon her.

An incredible sorrow welled up inside her, but she swallowed it, forced it away. Find the manuscript, she ordered herself. And then, what? Say goodbye? "I'm afraid."

"Of what?"

"There might have been a reason he hid this book. A real reason, not a paranoid fantasy." She shuddered. "What am I saying? I'm beginning to think like him."

He stroked her hair. "You aren't like your father."

"Oh, no? What if, because of his legacy, I can never have a sane relationship with a man? What if I can't have you?"

She felt him stiffen within her grasp, and she regretted her words. Pulling away from him, she turned her back and walked to the windows. Broken glass crunched beneath her espadrilles. "I'm sorry," she said. "I spoke out of turn. I'm not trying to force you into something you don't want."

"Nobody's forcing me, Mollie."

"Good. Because a relationship wouldn't work. You know that, don't you? You were right about the biography. And six months or a year from now, when you're finished . . . who knows what will happen by then?"

He wanted to tell her that he would come for her and they would live happily ever after. Desperately he wanted to comfort her, to make her understand how deeply he cared for her. But he would never hurt her with a promise that might not be fulfilled. He couldn't lie to her, and he didn't know what the future would bring for them.

"Mollie, you're not the only one who's confused. You're not the only one who's scared by the future."

"You? Why would you be scared?" She truly was surprised. Flynn always seemed so sure, so confident. "Why?"

"I don't want to lose you. Yesterday, when I couldn't find you, I almost went mad. I care deeply what happens to you. To us."

Us? Was there a future for them?

Her past and present collided in the room where she'd played with her father. Woodrow Locke seemed to be present, and he was smiling at her—not his cockeyed drunk smirk, but a kindly expression. He would have wanted her to be happy. And she missed him, wished she could share this moment with him, wished that Flynn could have spoken with him, asked him . . .

Through the dim shadows of the devastated playroom, Flynn approached her. He took both her hands in his.

"I love you, Mollie."

A sudden ringing in her ears deafened her. He loved her? Perhaps she'd misunderstood. But, no. His gentle gaze confirmed the words.

When his lips joined hers, she accepted this unbelievable event. He was truly there for her. For this splendid moment in time, he was hers.

"Flynn, I love you."

His arms tightened around her.

Nuzzling her ear, he murmured, "Let's go back to the boat."

"Let's finish searching here first."

"Forget it, I want to make love to you...."

Suddenly Mollie drew back. A memory was resurfacing.

"There was another game we used to play. Other than hide-and-seek," she said. "My father and I. I don't know why I haven't thought of it before."

"You'll think of it again. Let's make love."

Her gaze was sharp. Commanding green eyes focused on him. "It's about the manuscript. Maybe it's a clue."

"To hell with the manuscript."

"I don't believe you said that. *The Key* is so important to you."

"A cure for cancer is important. World peace is important. The love between a man and a woman is important." He smiled broadly. "Another book by Woodrow Locke is merely interesting."

She laughed delightedly and embraced him, knowing that she could adore this impatient, unpredictable man for a very long time. Nevertheless she had to tell him, "I want to pursue this thought before I forget it."

"As you wish." He kissed the tip of her nose. "What was this game?"

"My father would hide something, then he'd give me clues until I guessed where it was."

With endearing reluctance, he stepped away from her. "Give me an example of how it works."

"Okay. Sometimes the object itself would be a clue. Like hiding a ring inside the doorbell."

"*The Key,*" he said. "Locking doors and unlocking doors. Is there a special place where you kept keys?"

"On a hook by the door. Not a place where a manuscript could hide."

He rubbed his palms together, then frowned. "Could it be as obvious as hiding *The Key* here? On the Key where Woodrow Locke lived."

Slowly she nodded. "Seems blatant. But it makes sense. Perhaps that's why he arranged for me to inherit this house. But we still need to figure out where on the Key he hid *The Key*."

"Okay, let's think of words again. Manuscript," he said. "Script. Is there some kind of inscription anywhere?"

"The sundial? No, that's just numerals. And there's no address sign out front except on the mailbox." A sudden inspiration hit her. "My room. The wallpaper had flowers with their scientific names inscribed beneath them."

He bowed to her knowledge of the house. "Lead on, and I will follow."

As Mollie trooped down the narrow hallway to the foyer, her attitude was that of a lighthearted adventurer, and her honest excitement banished the remaining ghosts from the shadows. Amazing! She wasn't afraid anymore. The hacienda no longer seemed sinister. It was nothing more than a decrepit old house.

Flynn had said that he loved her. And she loved him, too. Though this joy might be short-lived, she was happy to seize the moment and to feel very, very good.

At the stairway, he caught her arm. "The stairs might be rotten. I'll go first."

"It's my house," she said. "I'm going first."

She placed her hand on the swooping iron banister and immediately withdrew it. "Yuck! This is covered with slime."

"Stay right here. I'll see what I can find to wipe it off."

As he went to search, Mollie tested a stair. It groaned beneath her foot, but seemed solid. She mounted one step. Then another. She was up four steps when Flynn returned with a rag.

"Nice job of waiting," he commented as he followed her and slapped the rag into her hand. "Hold onto the banister, please."

At the curve of the stairway, a step sagged precipitously under Mollie's weight, and she nimbly danced her way to the top. With greater care, Flynn climbed the remaining steps. "Remember that fifth one from the top. It's going to give out."

"This was my father's bedroom," she pointed to a closed door. "To the right is a little suite—Marianna's sitting room, bedroom and bath. Here are three more guest rooms."

"Why all the guest rooms?"

"No convenient motels. People who visited generally needed a bed. And my father loved visitors—drinking buddies and a new audience for his legendary stories about how he kept a crocodile in the basement and wrestled it to stay in shape."

Her childhood bedroom was the farthest on the left. The bed and dresser had been removed, but a small desk and several shelves remained. The white-and-green flowered-and-inscribed wallpaper had yellowed.

"Here we are. My inner sanctum." Louvered shutters covered the windows, and Mollie jiggled at one until it flipped open. Through a cracked window, she could see the pier and the fishing boat.

"It's ironic," she said. "I used to hide in here when outside, within my view, was the vast and beautiful sea."

He came up behind her and rested his hands on her shoulders. "But now, you can understand. Metaphorically, you've put your house in order. You've dealt with the pain and the rage."

"Nice metaphor, but I've only scratched the surface. Deep scratches, I'll grant you. But I'm afraid that it's going to take years to deal with the problems left over from my childhood." She shrugged. "Maybe I can do that while you're working on the biography. Find a shrink. Find a group. And emerge from my cocoon as a perfect butterfly."

"As long as you don't fly away."

"Never." She glanced around the room, rubbing her hands together. "Where to look. I always had secret hiding places. But in this room?" Her gaze scanned the wallpaper. Inscription? "I hid things in the dresser. And behind books on the shelves."

"What about the closet?" He opened the door and looked into a dank space with several empty hangers. "Nothing in here but a rancid odor."

"Not the closet," she said. "It was always a mess. I'd throw my clothes inside and slam the door."

"But you didn't hide this manuscript. Your father did. Do you think he'd put it in the closet?"

"Can you see up to the top shelf?"

Flynn stretched, but the upper shelf was slightly beyond his range. "Come here. I'll boost you up."

Mollie took a deep breath. The interior of the closet did smell foul. She stepped onto Flynn's laced fingers, and he lifted her up.

"Oh, my God." She clutched at his hair and shuddered. "There's a dead mouse up there."

With a leap, she was out of the closet, hopping around the room, making sour faces and shaking her hands to rid herself of the gross spectacle of a deceased rodent. Disgusting. "Why couldn't he have just buried his stupid treasure in the ground like any other self-respecting pirate?"

Flynn laughed. "I guess we ought to be grateful that Marianna and the Escobars have removed most of the furniture. At least we're not going to have to go through the old stuffing of beds and sofas."

"Couldn't we hire somebody to do this?"

"I doubt it. Who else is familiar with the intricate workings of your father's mind?"

"No one sane. And that probably includes me. Okay, where else should we poke around?"

"Loose floorboards?"

"Nope, there used to be a rug on this floor. One of those ugly green shags."

"Secret panels?"

"As far as I know, there aren't any. This isn't a medieval castle, you know. Just an old frame house."

"I've got it! There's got to be a crawl space."

"No way am I going into any crawl space."

"Script," he repeated. "Manuscript. Was there any other way he'd give you clues?"

"Sometimes, it was a musical clue. Like playing "A Glimpse of Stocking" meant he'd hidden something in my sock drawer. Or "Polly Put the Kettle On," meant it was behind the teapot in the kitchen. Or he'd make up a song."

From memory, Flynn hummed the tune she'd remembered in New York, "Longitude and latitude and the stuff about charts might be a reference to his boat."

"I hope not, because that boat's long gone." She paced the room. "Maybe it's a reference to a location, a property he owned. One of those dumb swamps."

"Your father might have been weird, Mollie, but he wasn't stupid. Nobody would hide a manuscript in a swamp and expect it to be found."

"Maybe he never expected it to be found. That would have been typical. He always cheated at hide-and-seek, and he loved to win. Maybe this is his final joke on me."

"What about the boat house?" Flynn suggested. "That's marginally connected to the idea of charts and maps with longitude and latitude."

"Marginally," she agreed. "But that's almost as ridiculous a hiding place as a swamp or a crawl space. It's sheer luck that the thing is still standing."

"Your father wouldn't have expected you to wait over ten years to make this search."

That was true. Mollie frowned. If she'd realized that she was the owner of this house, she surely would not have allowed it to go to ruin. Again, she thought, it was typical of her father to blunder into some silly hide-and-seek game while not taking care of his last will and testament, not arranging for things to be neat and tidy. Once again, from the grave, he'd left her with the mess.

"I don't want to search the boat house," she complained. "This house is bad enough, I'm sure the boat house is a condominium for dozens of nasty little creatures. And slime. And mildew."

Flynn shrugged. "You're right. But have you got any other brilliant ideas?"

"If only I could remember the second verse to that stupid song," she said. "That's probably the pertinent clue."

"There's a piano downstairs," Flynn suggested. "Want to play it again, Sam?"

She rolled her eyes. "Why not?"

Descending the stairs, Mollie carefully avoided the rickety fifth step from the top. It was the third step from the bottom that snapped when she placed her full weight upon it.

Her grip on the banister saved her from crashing all the way through. When she extricated her leg, the only damage was a bloody scratch from calf to ankle.

Before she could react with an angry string of curses, Flynn snatched her up in his arms and carried her the rest of the way down the stairs.

"Don't set me down on this filthy floor," she said. "I'm all right. I can stand."

He lowered her legs, and Mollie tested her weight. "I'm fine."

"That's a nasty cut." He went down onto one knee to inspect her leg. "Have you had tetanus shots lately?"

"I don't need one. I was cut by wood, not a rusty nail."

"You need a tetanus shot. And I'm taking you back to the boat and cleaning out that cut so it won't get infected. This is no time to be independent. I need to take care of you."

"I can take care of myself, thank you. And I do not wish to make another search of this disgusting house. Let's go to the piano and get this over with."

She hurried down the hallway toward the back room, forcing herself not to favor the injured leg. The scratch stung, but it wasn't a serious injury. Certainly not as serious as Flynn was assuming. Besides, she could handle physical pain.

When she approached the upright piano, she was glad for not turning back. Mollie sensed the impending discovery. Staring blankly, she lifted the keyboard cover. Her hand unconsciously reached for the ticktock metronome that used to stand on the top. She'd spent hours and hours practicing at this piano, playing until she thought her fingers would be paralyzed.

A strange warmth came over her. "I remember," Mollie said. "He wanted me to play that silly tune over and over. And he told me that someday, I would understand. Someday, I was to come here to this house and play the song for him."

Someday was now. She touched the ivory keys. The old piano squawked, horribly out of tune.

She struck the notes decisively. The second verse came easily, "From north and south, the endless degrees, when you only have to look ahead of your knees."

"That makes no sense," Flynn said.

"It doesn't have to, it's a nonsense verse." She reached to hit the high note, pinging heavily, and remembering how her father had showed her the metal strings inside the top of the piano. A hiding place? No, that wasn't quite right.

Her father had enjoyed her piano playing. She visualized his peaceful smile and played the song again—a silly ditty on an out-of-tune piano. Her foot reached for the pedal, encountering resistance. She couldn't put it down.

"It's here, Flynn! Inside the piano."

Mollie stepped back and watched as he lifted the lid on top of the upright, dislodging a mountain of mildew. "Not there," she said. "It's underneath. In front of my knees."

Together, they pried loose a warped wooden panel. Amid the filth that tumbled out was a large metal box, carefully wrapped in oilcloth.

Mollie gave a sharp cry when she saw it. With trembling fingers, she tore off the wrapping and opened the lid. The title page read, *Locke's Key*.

In her father's handwriting was a note, "I always loved you, Mollie."

She closed her eyes, feeling his presence all around her. "And I always loved you, Daddy...."

16

SHE PLACED *LOCKE'S KEY* in Flynn's hands. For once, she did not object to his reverence as he stroked the yellowed manuscript pages.

"I can't believe it," he said. "I can't believe I'm actually holding this."

"Why not? It's the treasure we've been hunting."

"Maybe I never really believed we'd find the thing. It'd been missing too long. Your memory wasn't good. There wasn't even a certainty that it even existed. I figured our odds at about a million to one."

"Then, why did you go through with this?"

"Because of the possibility. The incredible possibilities." He lifted the title page to read the first paragraph of text. His eyes scanned the first page, then the next. He murmured, "Your father was a hell of a craftsman. This makes his love poems to Ramona look like first drafts—exactly what they were. I still can't believe we've found it."

Somewhere inside herself, Mollie had always known that *Locke's Key* existed. Just as she'd always known that her father—despite his array of faults—loved her. The surprise was that she loved him, too.

Logically she shouldn't have. As a father, he'd screwed up in more ways than could be counted, and she'd told herself for years that she didn't care about him, didn't give a damn. But that wasn't true. She loved Woodrow Locke, that mean SOB who couldn't get through a single day without a drink, who had divorced her mother and abandoned Mollie, who had died before she had a chance to make her peace with him.

Now, the peace was hers. She no longer felt guilty about his problems, including his alcoholism, or her own emotional confusion. Mollie wasn't a bad or weak person. Her rage and fear and sorrow were twisted forms of her love. She could accept that. And face it.

When she gazed at Flynn, she knew she would not make the same mistakes in her future. Not in the name of love. Her worries about the future of their relationship vanished like the golden sunset over the Keys. Simply to love him was enough.

He looked up at her. "This story is about the two of you. A father and daughter who escape from a prison camp in World War II. They find sanctuary on an island, but he's disabled, paralyzed. And she has to take care of him." A sharp pain went through him. "This is your father's apology."

"Do you suppose it has a happy ending?"

"I hope so. You deserve the happiest ending."

She glided into his arms. With *Locke's Key* pressed between them, they kissed. His mouth had never been so honeyed to her taste. His nearness banished the rotting stench of the hacienda and reminded her of the roses he'd given her.

"Are you happy, Flynn?"

"I don't know," he said. "I feel more possessive than I ever have in my life. It's like I want to keep this manuscript for myself and not allow anyone else to read it."

"Like weirdo collectors who spend a fortune on a Rembrandt and then hang it in a secret basement?"

"Exactly." He grinned at her. "Sick, huh?"

"Indeed, it is."

"I feel the same way about you."

Purposely she misunderstood, "You want to hang me in a basement?"

"I want to keep you for myself, not to share you."

"Definitely sick."

As they retraced their steps to the front door, Mollie came to a decision. "I'm going to have this place repaired, put into order. And I'll live here. At least, for part of the year."

"What about your job?"

"I don't need it anymore," she pointed out. "I'm going to make a small fortune from the publication of *Locke's Key*. Plus, I've never exactly been poor. I received a significant inheritance from my mother's estate."

"You're an heiress, and I never knew?"

"I'm not superrich, but I've never needed to work. I had a job because I wanted to feel needed, competent. To fill up the hours of my life."

Together, they walked from the hacienda into the sunlight. Several yards clear of the house, Mollie took a deep breath of the fresh salty air. "I want Liana to visit me here. You remember her, don't you, Flynn?"

"The little girl from the Outreach program."

"Liana and lots of other children like her. This house was a great place to be a kid. And I never took advantage of it, because I was too busy mothering my father."

Her step was brisk and bouncy as she followed the single-file path around the house. There was only one thing missing from her future plans: her relationship with Flynn. Past the sundial, she brushed through the hibiscus hedges to the short pier and waited for him.

When he emerged from the shrubbery, she remembered the experiences they'd shared: his arrogance at the awards banquet; climbing up to the waterfall cave in

Colorado; cheesecake in New York; his stinky cigar; making love. He'd given her beautiful memories. These were times she would never forget.

His blue eyes met hers, and she responded. "You're fantastic," she said.

"Not I." He grasped her waist with his free hand. "You. And you are now coming with me onto the boat, so I can dress and bandage your leg."

"No bandage." But she went along with him toward the boat. "I feel grungy after being in that filth. I want a swim."

"Antiseptic first," he said.

After Flynn had carefully stored the manuscript in the dresser drawer of their sleeping cabin, he found a first aid kit in the tiny bathroom on the boat and instructed Mollie to place her leg on the small table. Her scratch wasn't as deep as he had feared, and he gently cleaned her supple calf with soap and water.

Though she winced when he applied the antiseptic, Flynn noticed a difference in her. Mollie was more relaxed than he'd ever seen her. She seemed to be looking forward to house renovations and changing her life. It hadn't escaped his attention that none of her plans included him.

If only the timing could be different. But now, more than ever, it was impossible for them to be together. Arranging for publication of *The Key* would take a tremendous amount of his time. And he had to make a start on the biography. Unlike Mollie, he would not receive royalties or advances on *Locke's Key*. He still had to devote a portion of his time to teaching and submitting enough of the biography to be paid for it.

Could he really ask her to wait? On the other hand, could he let her go?

When he started to dress her wound with a bandage, she pulled her leg away. "I want to swim."

"I'll put on another bandage when you get out of the water."

She reclaimed her unbandaged leg. "Obviously, you're a Ph.D. and not a medical doctor. Swim first and bandage later. And now I'm going to change into one of my barely worn swimsuits."

"Why?" he asked. "If you don't need a bandage, you don't need a bathing suit."

"But, Flynn—"

"I need to pull away from shore anyway, so we'll have deep enough water to swim."

"I am not skinny-dipping in broad daylight."

"I will, if you will."

With that enticement, he climbed the ladder to the deck and untied the boat from the pier. A hundred yards from the pier, he dropped anchor.

Shyly Mollie appeared from below deck. She clutched her green windbreaker around her. "Are you sure there's nobody around?"

"Positive." He peeled off his shorts and dived from the deck.

Before Mollie could follow, he shouted. "Wait!"

"What is it?" She squinted into the sun-sparkled waters.

"Nothing." He bobbed close to the boat. "I wanted a good look before you submerged."

"You're a voyeur, Flynn."

She made a shallow dive and came up near him. The gulf waters were as warm as a liquid caress. Mollie skimmed across the azure waves to Flynn. With a whoop, she pushed him under the water.

He disappeared, then surfaced behind her, tugging her legs so that she, too, was dunked. When he came after her again, imitating the music from *Jaws*, she splashed him.

"Stop it, Flynn."

"Make me."

"If you stop, I'll tell you a secret for your biography." He paused, treading water. "Yes?"

"My father was a clumsy swimmer," she revealed. "All he could manage was a dog paddle and a float."

As soon as she spoke, Flynn wished she hadn't. He didn't want to know her secrets. That was the whole reason for this separation. He didn't want to take advantage of her.

She splashed up close to him. "But I might be lying," she said. "You'll never know."

"I can find corroborating evidence. In spite of what Edleman thinks, I'm not a bad researcher." Flynn gave a whoop of triumph. "Edleman is going to die when he hears about *Locke's Key*."

"That's a very mature attitude, Dr. Carlson."

"Who needs mature. I won." He surged through the water, nearly embracing her. But he held back. "At least, I think I won."

"Come on, Flynn, let's swim."

They sliced through the water together, limber as dolphins and nearly synchronized in their ability. They swept in a wide arc and headed back toward the boat. When Mollie plunged up and down through the smoothly rippling waves, she felt clean and refreshed. And very much ready for lovemaking.

Flynn swam toward her, his shoulders churning the water like a sea god. The breeze tingled on her face, and she glided toward him.

Their naked bodies pressed together. The texture of damp hair on his chest tickled her smooth breasts. When they submerged in a kiss, his lips tasted of salt and their bodies buoyantly entwined.

He floated her to the surface. Holding onto the ladder from the boat, he lightly supported her back with his hands. The wetness of his lips on her skin mingled with the ocean's embrace and churned sensation through her entire body.

Cushioned by liquid azure, she did, indeed, feel like a mermaid. Their lovemaking took on a surreal mythic quality. Mollie closed her eyes, unable to distinguish between Flynn's teasing strokes and the caress of nature— the sun warmed her skin, the lapping waves rocked her and the light breeze raised her nipples to erection. She spread her thighs in response to his touch. When his fingers parted her delicate flesh and glided inside her, she felt as if she were being tantalized by the sea.

Yet it was Flynn she wanted. Not a mysterious, ephemeral Adonis. But a real man with real complications and confusion and demands. "I want you inside me, Flynn. I want you to be a part of me."

They climbed onto the boat, the home of their loving. In the sleeping cabin, Mollie returned the attention Flynn had lavished upon her, delicately manipulating his flat hard nipples, stroking his erection and guiding him into her.

When he entered her, his expression was ecstatic, and he murmured, "I love you, Mollie. So much."

"Tell me again."

"I love you."

He confirmed his vow with a hot, driving passion that sent her senses whirring.

"I love you," she cried out. "Love you, love you."

As she clutched him against her, Mollie wished the moment would never end. She wanted him to stay with her, to be with her forever. Yet, that was not to be. They would go their ways, as they'd planned from the start.

He had never promised more, and she was strangely content with that. Their love was commitment enough.

As they lay side by side, their long bodies stretched out on the small cabin bed, Mollie felt peaceful. Not hurt.

"Would you mind," he asked, "if I had a cigar?"

"I would mind. This cabin is too small."

"Would you mind if we went up on deck and I had a cigar? I want to celebrate."

It seemed an innocent enough request. Without a stitch of clothing, they went on deck and lay in the tropical sun.

When Flynn lit up his fat cigar, she laughed.

"What's so funny?"

"You are," she said. "I've never seen a naked man with a cigar before."

"It's different," he conceded. "But I'm a real adventurous kind of guy, if you haven't happened to notice. And this has been a landmark day."

"Why is that, O great adventurer?"

"We've found the missing manuscript of one of the great American writers. Plus, more importantly, I've told a mermaid that I loved her."

"Today's important for me, too."

They sat quietly, basking.

"I don't want to be apart from you," he said. "Not for a day."

"It won't be forever."

"We make a good team." He cleared his throat. "I've never been in love before. Not like this. I will come back to you. Wait for me."

She turned her mysterious green-eyed gaze upon him. Her expression was solemn. "I'd better leave you now."

"Not yet. In a few more hours."

"Now. We can't be together while you're writing the biography. You were right about that, Flynn. I don't want a relationship where I'm being used—consciously or unconsciously. But we're both on the verge of forgetting that. I don't want to make a mistake."

She rose up from the deck, and her naked, unself-conscious loveliness caused a poignant ache within him. He couldn't be separated from her. His life would be empty without her.

But she was right, and he had to accept her judgment. Their love would have to wait a bit longer. He rose to his feet. "I'll fire up the engine. Where should I take you?"

"Back to shore. I want to stay here on Stamper Key for a while. Maybe when you return the boat to Marianna, you could arrange for Rafael to come pick me up."

She went below deck, found her suitcase and began to pack. The unmade bed in the small sleeping cabin was still scented with their lovemaking. Mingled with the fragrance of roses.

The fishing boat was moving, slowly churning through the sea toward the pontoon pier outside her father's hacienda. She was sorry that their adventure was almost over. Their loving had been beautiful. Perhaps, someday, it would be again.

She returned to the deck, fully dressed and carrying her suitcase. Meeting Flynn at the helm, she said, "I've left a few things that wouldn't fit in my suitcase. Could you send them to Marianna's house?"

"I'll bring them in person," he promised.

"No, that's not wise. We shouldn't plan to see each other every week. Not until you've finished your biography."

"But, Mollie—"

"No."

She tossed her suitcase onto the pier and climbed after it. She raised her hand and slowly waved to him. "Goodbye, Flynn. I love you."

He returned to the helm of the boat and saluted her. "I'll be back, Mollie. Count on it. I'll be back before you know it."

While the fishing boat chugged away from the pier, Mollie felt her eyes fill with hot tears. She already missed him. There would be a black hole in her life until he returned to her. But she'd learn to live with it.

As she watched, the boat stopped. The engine went dead.

Flynn was shouting something indecipherable and waving his arms like a madman.

"What?" She ran to the very end of the pier. "What?"

Fully dressed, he dived from the boat and swam toward her. When the waters were too shallow for swimming, he charged through them, splashing until he reached the pier and stood waist deep in the water below her. He flung his arms wide. "Marry me, Mollie."

"What are you saying?"

"I'm saying that I want to spend the rest of my life with you. Starting right now and lasting until the end of time."

"But the biography?"

"The hell with it. The world doesn't need another Woodrow Locke biography." He held his hand up to her. "Please, Mollie. Say you'll be my wife."

Though physically yearning for him, she held back. "I can't ask you to give up the biography. You're the right person to write it. Maybe you're the only person who could write it."

"I don't think so." He laughed and sloshed a shimmering wave toward her. "You should write it, Mollie. You're the only person."

The absolute truth of his statement struck her immediately.

"My God, you're right." She knelt on the pier. "You'll help me, won't you? I mean—*if* I decide to write it. I'll need to think about it...."

He caught both her hands in his. "Only if you marry me."

"With pleasure."

With a tug, he pulled her into the water beside him and enfolded her in an embrace. "My darling mermaid. I love you."

"I love you, Flynn."

Mollie kissed him full on the lips. Finally her search was truly over. With Flynn at her side, Mollie believed in the future. She believed in love that could last forever—one day at a time—without secrets and without fear.

He had unlocked her heart. Together, they were free.

HARLEQUIN Temptation

COMING NEXT MONTH

#309 AFTER HOURS Gina Wilkins

Executive assistant Angelique St. Clair knew the office gossips said she and her boss, Rhys Wakefield, were made for each other; they were both cold, intimidating workaholics. And maybe they were—during business hours. But after hours, the heat they generated was enough to melt a polar ice cap . . . and the heart of one very cool CEO!

#310 TALISMAN Laurien Berenson

Woodbury, Connecticut, wasn't New York City. And Kelly Ransome wasn't a city woman. She was straightforward and freshly scrubbed . . . and came equipped with three Dobermans! But that didn't stop journalist Eric Devane from pursuing her. After all, Eric had an overexuberant Rotweiller pup on his hands, and Kelly was a dog trainer— the best. And Eric Devane *only* pursued the best.

#311 HIDDEN MESSAGES Regan Forest

Vacationing on a Scottish isle, Laurie MacDonald fell in love with Eric Sinclair—part Gypsy, part rogue and all sex appeal. But then she discovered his love was a deception and she plotted a fitting revenge . . . only she couldn't convince her heart she was better off without him.

#312 ALWAYS Jo Morrison

Tanner McNeil wanted a wife. After eight years of trying to convince footloose Jodi to settle down with him on the farm, he'd given up. Meeting Lara Jamison restored his hope in happy endings. But Lara suspected that perfect as they were for each other in bed, Tanner was still seeing Jodi in his dreams. . . .

HARLEQUIN
American Romance®

THE LOVES OF A CENTURY

Join American Romance in a nostalgic look back at the twentieth century—at the lives and loves of American men and women from the turn-of-the-century to the dawn of the year 2000.

Journey through the decades from the dance halls of the 1900s to the discos of the seventies . . . from Glenn Miller to the Beatles . . . from Valentino to Newman . . . from corset to miniskirt . . . from beau to significant other.

Relive the moments . . . recapture the memories.

Watch for all the CENTURY OF AMERICAN ROMANCE titles in Harlequin American Romance. In one of the four American Romance books appearing each month, for the next ten months, we'll take you back to a decade of the twentieth century, where you'll relive the years and rekindle the romance of days gone by.

Don't miss a day of A CENTURY OF AMERICAN ROMANCE.

A CENTURY OF
AMERICAN ROMANCE
1910s

The women . . . the men . . . the passions . . . the memories . . .

Nicole had a second chance . . . to live.

One moment Nicole was standing in the deli's doorway, smiling at the handsome oceanographer. The next, she reached out to stop the gunman who'd jumped out of the rain-shrouded Manhattan day.

But when Nicole awoke, it was early morning August 30, a full week earlier. Had she been dreaming? Doubt grew stronger as the day unfolded—a day she remembered before it had even begun. Then she again met the oceanograher—David Germaine—and her world shifted on its axis.

David was her desire, her destiny, her only hope of averting disaster. Could this memorable stranger help her reverse fate? Meantime, dark forces gathered. . . .

Don't miss this exciting Harlequin Intrigue coming this July wherever Harlequins are sold. . . . Watch for #142 *Déjà Vu* by Laura Pender!

HI-142-1

Harlequin Superromance®

A powerful restaurant conglomerate that draws the best and brightest to its executive ranks. Now almost eighty years old, Vanessa Hamilton, the founder of Hamilton House, must choose a successor.
Who will it be?

Matt Logan: He's always been the company man, the quintessential team player. But tragedy in his daughter's life and a passionate love affair made him make some hard choices....

Paula Steele: Thoroughly accomplished, with a sharp mind, perfect breeding and looks to die for, Paula thrives on challenges and wants to have it all . . . but is this right for her?

Grady O'Connor: Working for Hamilton House was his salvation after Vietnam. The war had messed him up but good and had killed his storybook marriage. He's been given a second chance—only he doesn't know what the hell he's supposed to do with it....

Harlequin Superromance invites you to enjoy Barbara Kaye's dramatic and emotionally resonant miniseries about mature men and women making life-changing decisions. Don't miss:

- CHOICE OF A LIFETIME—a July 1990 release.
- CHALLENGE OF A LIFETIME
  —a December 1990 release.
- CHANCE OF A LIFETIME—an April 1991 release.

COMING SOON

In September, two worlds will collide in four very special romance titles. Somewhere between first meeting and happy ending, Dreamscape Romance will sweep you to the very edge of reality where everyday reason cannot conquer unlimited imagination—or the power of love. The timeless mysteries of reincarnation, telepathy, psychic visions and earthbound spirits intensify the modern lives and passion of ordinary men and women with an extraordinary alluring force.

Available in September!

EARTHBOUND—Rebecca Flanders
THIS TIME FOREVER—Margaret Chittenden
MOONSPELL—Regan Forest
PRINCE OF DREAMS—Carly Bishop

DRSC-RR